W9-BSH-715

"Give me the baby," the gunman demanded.

"No," Macy said, holding Addie more closely.

The baby cried again, and tears appeared in her eyes. The poor thing. Could she sense the danger in the air? If Tanner wasn't here now, he must be hurt. The only way he'd let this confrontation happen was over his dead body. The thought caused Macy's heart to lurch into her throat.

Moisture tried to rush to her eyes, but she held it back. This fight wasn't over. Not yet.

"Did you say no?"

Macy pulled Addie closer. "Stay away from her."

The man's eyes narrowed. "You don't know what you're getting into, lady."

"You're a monster."

"I'll show you a monster if you don't hand over the girl."

"No," Macy repeated.

"Have it your way." He raised his gun toward Macy...

Christy Barritt's books have won a Daphne du Maurier Award for Excellence in Suspense and Mystery and have been twice nominated for an RT Reviewers' Choice Best Book Award. She's married to her Prince Charming, a man who thinks she's hilarious—but only when she's not trying to be. Christy's a self-proclaimed klutz, an avid music lover and a road-trip aficionado. For more information, visit her website at christybarritt.com.

Books by Christy Barritt

Love Inspired Suspense

Keeping Guard
The Last Target
Race Against Time
Ricochet
Desperate Measures
Hidden Agenda
Mountain Hideaway
Dark Harbor
Shadow of Suspicion
The Baby Assignment

THE BABY ASSIGNMENT

CHRISTY BARRITT

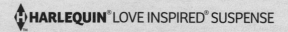

HARLEQUIN® LOVE INSPIRED® SUSPENSE

If you purchased this book without a cover you should be aware that this book is stolen property. It was reported as "unsold and destroyed" to the publisher, and neither the author nor the publisher has received any payment for this "stripped book."

Recycling programs
for this product may
not exist in your area.

LOVE INSPIRED BOOKS

ISBN-13: 978-1-335-54350-9

The Baby Assignment

Copyright © 2018 by Christy Barritt

All rights reserved. Except for use in any review, the reproduction or utilization of this work in whole or in part in any form by any electronic, mechanical or other means, now known or hereinafter invented, including xerography, photocopying and recording, or in any information storage or retrieval system, is forbidden without the written permission of the editorial office, Love Inspired Books, 195 Broadway, New York, NY 10007 U.S.A.

This is a work of fiction. Names, characters, places and incidents are either the product of the author's imagination or are used fictitiously, and any resemblance to actual persons, living or dead, business establishments, events or locales is entirely coincidental.

This edition published by arrangement with Love Inspired Books.

® and TM are trademarks of Love Inspired Books, used under license. Trademarks indicated with ® are registered in the United States Patent and Trademark Office, the Canadian Intellectual Property Office and in other countries.

www.Harlequin.com

Printed in U.S.A.

To everything there is a season,
and a time to every purpose under the heaven:
A time to be born, and a time to die; a time to plant,
and a time to pluck up that which is planted;
A time to kill, and a time to heal;
a time to break down, and a time to build up;
A time to weep, and a time to laugh;
a time to mourn, and a time to dance.
—Ecclesiastes 3:1-4

This book is dedicated to all the moms out there
who sacrifice so much for their children.

ONE

Macy Mills froze as a shadow filled her office doorway. She dropped the colorful foam blocks she used as part of play therapy as her instincts alerted her that trouble had arrived.

She glanced up. When Macy's gaze met the eyes of the man there, she sucked in a breath.

It wasn't her next client standing at the door; nor was it a coworker. No, all her colleagues here at the psychotherapy center were at a birthday lunch.

Instead, the man who'd crushed Macy's heart five years ago lingered in the doorway, his frame filling the space entirely.

As he stood there in his cowboy glory, she remembered all his charm and his Southern drawl. A package that had been alluring at one time.

"Tanner Wilson," she muttered.

"Macy." He nodded, offering a terse, professional greeting. His voice sounded cool and distant, the opposite of how he'd sounded when they'd been together. Back then, there'd been a tenderness and warmth that was reserved just for her.

The absence of those traits reminded Macy of how much had changed between the two of them, even though it seemed like just yesterday they were incredibly happy together. All those memories rushed back to her like a flood that left her nearly drowning.

Macy took a good look at him. Tanner had always been tall, but now he was broader. More muscular maybe? Beneath his cowboy hat, brown wavy hair with golden highlights peeked out. He wore his typical jeans with a black T-shirt and cowboy boots.

Valor and arrogance blended into one appealing, gorgeous bundle.

Except something was different.

He was holding a...baby.

Macy stood and blinked, certain her eyes were deceiving her.

A baby? But...

Her heart lurched at the picture they painted together. Had Tanner come here to gloat? To remind Macy about the kind of life they could have had together if everything hadn't fallen apart?

She rubbed her throat, trying to control her words and not give away the fact that she still harbored hurt deep inside. She had to draw on every ounce of professional strength inside her as old dreams of a forever family surged to the surface.

"What a surprise to see you here," she finally croaked out.

"It was a surprise for me also to learn you were back in the area." Tanner's words sounded dull, and Macy knew that he wasn't here for social reasons or to rehash the past. He needed her for something and obligation had led him to her door.

"Here I am." Macy's voice cracked as she said the words. So much for acting like the cultured, educated woman she was. She felt like an insecure high schooler who'd just bumped into her crush.

Macy had envisioned many times what it would be like if she and Tanner ever ran into each other again. This was not what she'd pictured: her on the floor sanitizing blocks, smelling like Clorox, and showing the effects of a poor night's sleep due to drinking caffeine too late while meeting a friend for coffee. And there was Tanner, looking like the picture of strength and masculinity as he tenderly held a baby.

Years of tumultuous history stretched taut between them.

Macy drew in a deep breath, stepped closer and rubbed the back of the baby girl's hand with her finger. She offered a smile reserved just for the child, who stared back at Macy with wide brown eyes. The baby's skin felt so soft beneath hers, and Macy's pulse pounded in her ears as unfulfilled longings rose in her.

Especially when she looked at Tanner holding the child.

The girl was probably six months old and adorable with dark brown hair holding a touch of curl. She shoved her hand in her mouth, drooling slightly, and totally oblivious to the tension around her.

"Who's this?" Macy asked.

"She's why I'm here," Tanner said.

Macy could feel the tension radiating from him. Something was wrong. Something more than seeing Macy again.

"She's the only reason I'm here," Tanner clarified.

There'd always been something about a big strong man holding a delicate baby that did something to Macy's insides, sending them tumbling into a pit of warm and gooey sap. That made her want to abandon all her professional aspirations and simply be a mom. It was all she'd ever wanted to be.

She cleared her throat, shoving those thoughts aside. With every day she inched closer to thirty, those yearnings became more like a distant dream that would never be realized. She'd accepted that and settled for being married to her job instead.

He glanced down the hallway behind him before lowering his voice. "I know it's been a while, but can we talk, Macy?"

Dread pooled in her stomach. Was this baby his? Was she going to have to face the reality that Tanner had gone on without her? That another woman had taken his heart captive when Macy had been unable to claim the honor?

Macy wasn't sure if she could handle that.

She'd thought she was stronger than this, but she wasn't. Her degrees or accomplishments didn't matter. Sometimes heartache still superseded good sense, however hard she fought it.

"I suppose." She stepped aside and allowed him fully into her office. Once inside, she shut the door to give them some privacy, even though everyone else was gone.

She pointed to the couch against the wall. A cheerful red carpet, shaggy and casual, stretched in front of it, along with colorful pillows on the floor and some plants to soften the whole room and make it more welcoming.

"Have a seat." Macy pointed to the couch and lowered herself there.

Tanner sat beside her and turned the baby so that the infant faced Macy.

"She's just precious." Macy knew she was killing time and delaying whatever inevitable conversation they would have. Leaving Tanner a letter five years ago wasn't the most sensitive or wisest thing she could have done. But what other choice had she had? If she'd seen his eyes, she would have changed her mind, and she couldn't do that.

"Her name is Addie," Tanner said. "She was left at the FBI office."

The FBI. She should have known. It had always been Tanner's dream to work there. The most important thing he could achieve. His highest goal in life.

More important than anything, including Macy.

She forced herself to remain focused and not let that familiar old bitterness creep into her psyche. "There was no clue about who she is?"

"Addie's mom told the security guard at the gates to our field office that the baby needed protection and that she had no one else to turn to. She also said that if she kept Addie with her, they'd kill her."

The words chilled Macy. "That's it? No idea of who 'they' would be?"

Tanner shook his head. "No idea. Not a lot to go on, right?"

"Not at all. Any belongings?"

"A diaper bag. That's where we found your name. It was scribbled on a piece of paper we located in one of the pockets."

She sucked in a breath, uncertain if she'd heard correctly. "My name?"

Tanner nodded and showed her a grainy

black-and-white photo of a woman wearing a baseball cap and oversize sweatshirt. The woman's head remained down. "Recognize her?"

She studied the photo, searching her thoughts for a clue to this woman's identity. The picture didn't give her any leads. It was too hard to clearly identify any of her features.

"I can't say I do," Macy said. "Not from this photo, at least. I have an average of thirty clients a week. Some I see once a week, some every other week, some once a month."

"I understand."

Macy shook her head again and glanced at the picture once more. "I wish I had some answers for you, Tanner. I really do."

"So do we."

Macy shifted, processing what he'd told her. "Despite the fact that my name was found in the diaper bag, I'm fairly confident I don't know this woman. I'd certainly remember Addie."

"She's my latest assignment."

A hint of amusement sparked in Macy's gaze as she remembered the time she and Tanner had babysat her niece and nephew for a day. Tanner had started strong, but had ended frazzled and exhausted. The big tough guy could do a lot of things, but chasing children and changing diapers wasn't his forte.

"Really?" She licked her lips and kept her tone neutral.

Humor lingered in his gaze, but only for a moment. "You don't have to pretend that this scenario is ideal. I know I'm not a natural."

"A lot could have changed in five years. Maybe you have a whole gaggle of children at home now." Remorse pounded at her temples. She still mourned for the loss of their relationship, and part of her didn't want to know if her guess was the truth.

Something unreadable flickered in Tanner's gaze. "I don't."

Macy wished the proclamation didn't bring her a touch of delight. Thinking of him being happy with someone else twisted her gut in ways it shouldn't. He was no longer hers, and he never would be.

Tanner shifted, looking ill at ease—something that he rarely ever was. "We're all aware that this case is obviously bigger than we understand. We need your help figuring out who the mother is. The sooner we learn her identity, the sooner we can find some answers. Maybe you'll recall something."

"I don't know, Tanner..." She swallowed hard, the words burning a hole in her gut. The thought of working with Tanner was almost more than she could stomach. Instinctively, she reached forward and stroked Addie's hand again. "I really don't know how I can help."

"Go through your clients. Both here and in Oklahoma. See if anyone matches. Talk to your colleagues."

"Of course. I can do that." Relief washed through her. She could do that alone—without Tanner. She could handle that much more easily than having to interact face-to-face with Tanner. "When do you need my response?"

"Now."

"Now?" She let out a laugh, all her momentary relief disappearing. "I have an appointment in an hour and two more after that. I—"

Tanner leveled his gaze with her, his baby blues locking onto hers. "I know, Macy. I'm sorry to ask you this. You know I wouldn't unless—"

"Unless you were desperate," she finished. They'd both ended things on a bitter note. Neither would purposefully seek the other out unless it couldn't be avoided. That was obviously the case right now.

Tanner frowned but nodded.

Macy rubbed her hands across her pants, trying to collect her thoughts and sort out each of the demanding priorities facing her. "I'll need at least a day. I can't just cancel on my clients. And it's going to take time."

"We don't have a lot of time. We believe this baby and her mother are in danger."

Her responsibilities clashed inside her. Macy had an obligation to her clients—some were on the verge of breakdowns. Many were at the end of their ropes. But she could see the urgency of this situation as well.

"I understand," she said. "I can work all night. You have to be aware that I have clients who will face crises if I don't meet with them. I'd be happy to dedicate myself to this when those appointments are done."

"Thank you." Apology stained his eyes. Or was it regret? Bitterness?

Working with Tanner—knowing she'd have to face him again, even if just for a few minutes—would be challenging. She hadn't seen him in years. And it was better that way, with the distance and separation between them. There was too much water under the bridge. Too much had transpired between them, and it all added up to a world of hurt.

"Of course." She fluffed a pillow, desperate to distract herself from the scent of his leathery aftershave. She hadn't realized until this moment just how much she'd missed it. Craved it, for that matter.

"I'll check back in with you tomorrow and see if you discovered anything."

She nodded stiffly at the idea of seeing him again. It was something she'd never get used to. "Of course."

He stood, Addie grabbing his finger as his form dwarfed Macy. He waved the baby's hand back and forth, looking like a natural, despite how uncomfortable and ill-equipped he claimed to be.

"I think you're underestimating yourself." Macy stood also and gave Addie's foot another gentle squeeze. "You'd do fine with a baby."

A frown tugged at the corner of his mouth. "I can keep the baby safe physically. But I have no idea how to take care of an infant. This isn't exactly in my job description."

Macy didn't want to debate with him about whether or not he was qualified. Instead, she needed some space from him—and soon. "Let me walk you to the door."

Quietly, they walked down the hallway, through the office, and toward the front entrance.

Why had a mom abandoned her baby at the FBI office? The maternal bond was exceptionally strong, so what had made her so desperate? Macy didn't have time to think too much further about it now. Her thoughts were racing all over the place since she'd first seen Tanner at her door.

They paused in the waiting room. The office wasn't very large. There were five psychologists here and three administrative staff members. They all felt like family and often spent weekends doing cookouts at each other's houses.

The place had recently been redecorated in subtle shades of blue and brown—colors that promoted serenity. A saltwater aquarium, another object that calmed people down, was placed strategically in the corner, and soothing music usually played overhead.

Macy glanced outside and saw an agent standing at the door. Tanner followed her gaze.

"My partner," Tanner explained.

As Tanner turned to her, Addie let out a cry. Macy saw the flash of panic on Tanner's face. He bounced the baby in his arms, talking in soothing tones.

"It's going to be okay," he murmured. "Nothing's going to happen to you. I promise."

Macy's very bones ached at his tender words. He would have been a good father. If only...

No, she couldn't think about that.

"We'll talk tomorrow," she assured him.

The last thing she wanted to do was prolong the amount of time she spent with Tanner. It would be too painful, not something she wanted to endure. She would find the answers, be done with this, and hopefully never have to see him again.

As she opened her mouth to say goodbye, a noise outside drew her ear. Was that...a gunshot? She sucked in a quick breath.

Tanner visibly tensed beside her and reached

for his gun. Before he could grab it, she heard a groan outside.

Tanner's partner fell to the ground.

The next instant, three men wielding military-grade guns and wearing ski masks burst into the building.

Tanner grabbed Macy and rushed toward the hallway. He pushed her inside the first room he came to and quickly scanned it. Good. No windows.

He thrust Addie into Macy's arms, apprehension welling in him at the gravity of the situation. "Stay here. Lock the door. Get in a closet. Understand?"

He didn't have time to rationalize or reassure her. All they could focus on now was survival. Time was of the essence.

Macy's eyes widened, but she nodded, looking shell-shocked.

He gripped her shoulder. "You're strong. You can do this."

Before she could say anything else, he shut the door and waited until he heard the lock click in place. Then he ducked behind a corner, careful to remain covered. Footsteps pounded toward him in the distance.

A bullet whizzed through the air, hitting the wall in front of him. Tanner fired back, missing the shooter by mere inches.

More footsteps scrambled in the waiting room.

Another bullet hit the plaster behind him. He had to put an end to this. It had been risky bringing Addie out today, but Tanner had followed procedure. That procedure had gone totally wrong, unfortunately.

Lord, please keep Macy and Addie safe. Please. He'd never forgive himself if they were hurt on his watch.

In an instant, both Macy and Addie's faces flashed through his head. Despite his history with Macy, he still felt an unusual surge of protectiveness about her.

His presence here could have put her in danger, and he couldn't live with himself if something happened to her because of him. Even if the woman had left him and turned his life upside down.

He peered around the corner again and raised his gun. The smoky, acidic smell of ammunition filled the air as this place of healing became a place of violence. The irony hit him, but he couldn't linger on it now.

A masked gunman ducked for cover behind a plush chair. The man popped up when he spotted Tanner. Before the man could take a shot, Tanner fired. The assailant yelped and fell out of sight.

Tanner knew this was far from over, though.

Where were the other gunmen? Just what were they planning?

He grabbed his phone and called his office. "Immediate backup needed. We've got an active shooter situation at the Third Day Psychotherapy Center. Three gunmen."

"Backup is en route."

Before Tanner hung up, another gunman stepped out from behind the glass-enclosed reception area and raised his gun. The bullet grazed Tanner's biceps.

He flinched but ignored the pain. Instead, he fired back, hitting his target on the shoulder. The man groaned and retreated.

Silence stretched through the air.

Who were these guys? They shot like professionals, like people who had experience. And that fact didn't settle well with Tanner.

He assumed Addie's mom was fleeing from a domestic situation, an abusive boyfriend or husband. But if this current incident was connected with Addie—and he believed it was—then this was much bigger than he'd surmised.

Slowly, Tanner crept toward the waiting room. He had to see what was going on out there and try to get a read on things. As his foot hit broken glass, he looked down. A trail of blood led to the back exit.

Had all of them retreated or just one?

Remaining close to the wall, Tanner continued to check the area. He had to make sure everything was clear before he went to get Macy and Addie. He wouldn't relax until he saw them again and knew they were safe.

Just then, another bullet shattered the silence of the room. The fish tank behind him exploded, and water gushed to the floor.

Tanner dove behind the couch, his pulse pounding in his ears. This place was a battle zone.

He glanced at the office door where he'd placed Macy and the baby. At least he knew no one had gone in there. They were safe. He planned on keeping it that way.

Another thought rammed into his mind.

What if there was another way into that office? What if those gunmen had only been a distraction while another man went after Addie and the woman he'd once loved?

TWO

Macy froze beside the heavy wooden desk as silence stretched outside the room where she and Addie were hidden.

She'd heard the gunfire. The shouts. But she had no idea what was going on out there. She had no way of finding out—unless she opened a door, which she had no desire to do.

Tanner probably hadn't realized there were two doors that led into the room, and she hadn't had the chance to tell him. He'd probably assumed the other doorway was a closet. In reality, it connected this office with the reception area.

Leaving Addie on the floor, Macy had locked that door and shoved a bookshelf in front of it. Would it be enough? She prayed it was because she was out of options in here.

A slight noise caught her ear, and she raised her head high enough to peer over the top of the desk.

Her gaze stopped at the door that was partial

blocked by the bookshelf. The door handle jiggled ever-so-slightly.

Her breath caught.

That wasn't Tanner. Or was it? No, he would announce himself.

She gripped the edge of the desk, hardly able to breathe. Fear rippled up her spine, fear like she'd never felt before. How was she going to protect Addie if these gunmen confronted her? She had nothing to defend herself with. Nothing that would stop them. Macy had no doubt they would kill her if she stood in their way.

She swallowed hard. She didn't want it to come to that, but she'd do whatever necessary to protect this child, even if it meant sacrificing herself in the process.

Who were these men? She assumed they were connected with Addie. It was the only thing that made sense to her. But she supposed they could in some way be tied with the counseling center. An angry client suffering with a psychotic break maybe. It had happened before, though never to this extreme.

It didn't matter right now.

Survival was the only thing that was important.

She glanced beside her. She'd placed Addie out of sight beneath a heavy wooden desk. The baby lay on the carpet there, oblivious to danger but getting agitated by the minute. Thankfully the child hadn't screamed amidst the commotion. It made Macy wonder if Addie was accustomed to chaos and unaffected by it. Children had the amazing ability to cope throughout life's traumas.

Thank goodness she couldn't crawl yet. Macy hoped the baby was safer there, out of sight, than in her arms. Macy remained beside her, comforting her. Praying. Warding away worst-case scenarios.

Her back ached as she hunched over. Her legs cramped from the confined quarters. But those things were the least of her worries.

This wasn't ideal. None of it was. But Macy couldn't stand out in the middle of the room like an open target.

And she could no longer just stay here defenseless. Certainly there was something in this room she could use as a makeshift weapon. There had to be.

Before she could lose her courage, she scrambled out from her hiding place. With trembling hands, she opened the door to the supply cabinet behind her.

She scanned the shelves there. Was there anything she could defend herself with? A stapler? Not ideal. She picked up a bottle of toner, and an idea fluttered through her mind.

She ducked back under the desk, unscrewed the cap on top, and waited.

Her stomach clenched tighter and tighter with each second that passed. What was happening on the other side of that door?

Addie let out a little squeal, and Macy tried to shush her. The sound was so sweet and such a contrast to the dangerous intensity of the moment. Macy wanted to relish the sound, to absorb it and the innocence it emanated. But this wasn't the time.

She held her breath, listening, trying to anticipate what would happen next.

Another round of gunfire exploded outside.

Tanner…had Tanner been hurt? She didn't care about the man anymore, but she didn't him to be injured…or worse.

She closed her eyes and tried to control her breathing. Tried to use the techniques she taught others who suffered with anxiety. Tried to visualize positive outcomes.

You can do this, Macy. You're smart and capable.

But the mind had always been her battleground, not her office space. Not guns or violence. Her weapons were self-control. Faith. Reprogramming thoughts. Prayer.

A surge of anxiety rose in her, and she gripped the toner more tightly.

Shouts sounded outside.

What was going on? Part of her hated hiding out, while the other part was too terrified to move.

All of this over a baby? That's what her mind kept going back to and tried to wrap itself around.

Every child was important...but what made Addie such a commodity to someone that they'd go to these lengths?

Or maybe this wasn't about Addie at all, she reminded herself. It could be related to one of her other cases, one of her clients. There was so much she didn't know, but she was certain that she had to protect this child.

"It's going to be okay, precious," she whispered. She gently poked the baby's stomach, and Addie kicked her legs, temporarily distracted from her growing agitation. "We're going to get things figured out for you. Somehow. Some way."

We? She meant Tanner. Tanner would figure this out. Macy would do whatever she could to help, but this was above her skill level.

Just then, she heard something scraping against the floor.

The shelf, she realized.

Someone had gotten the door open and was now shoving the bookshelf out of the way.

The scraping sound stopped.

That meant someone was inside the room with her.

The skin on the back of her neck crawled.

Macy gripped the toner more tightly. If only she could see what was happening.

She put a finger over her lips, urging Addie to remain quiet. As if the baby could understand.

She lowered her head, trying to peek through the crack between the desk and the floor. She saw black combat boots headed her way.

She sucked in a quick breath.

It was one of the gunmen.

Her blood went cold.

Her heart pounded furiously into her ears as she pushed herself deeper under the desk. No, no, no...

Please, baby Addie. Stay quiet.

The baby was getting tired and irritated. It was probably time for her to eat. Or her gums could hurt with incoming teeth. Or her diaper could need to be changed.

From his current angle, the man couldn't see them. But the farther he came into the room, Macy knew the gunman would spot her. And when he did...

She shuddered as scenarios rushed through her mind.

He stepped closer, closer. Footsteps padded on carpet. Macy could hear him breathing, his inhales and exhales heavy and laced with adrenaline. Danger crackled in the air.

She put a hand on Addie's chest as the baby's lips pulled downward like she might cry.

Macy held her breath, hardly able to hear over the blood rushing in her ears.

You can do this. You can do this.

She sensed the gunman was closer. Only seconds away from spotting her.

Just then, Addie let out a whimper.

Macy had to take action. The gunman's footsteps quickened, headed her way. She waited until his shadow blocked the light above her.

Then she sprang from beneath the desk and flung the toner at him. Powder went into his eyes, and he howled with pain, bending over and turning in a partial circle.

Quickly, Macy grabbed Addie, climbed from her hiding spot, and rushed toward the doorway. Before she got there, the man growled, "Stop right there."

His voice chilled her to the bone.

Macy turned, anxiety stretching through each of her muscles. She kept Addie shielded and looked over her shoulder.

Dear Lord, please protect us.

The man wiped his eyes with one hand, but he held his gun with the other. The barrel was pointed straight at her. Malice stained his gaze as he stared at her and blood oozed from his shoulder.

"Give me the baby," he demanded.

"No," Macy said, holding Addie more closely. The baby whined again, and tears appeared in her eyes. The poor thing. Could she sense the danger in the air? Her agitation only compounded Macy's stress.

If Tanner wasn't here now, he must be hurt. The only way he'd let this confrontation happen was over his dead body. The thought caused a lump to form in Macy's throat.

Moisture tried to rush to her eyes, but she held it back. This fight wasn't over. Not yet.

"Did you say no?"

Macy pulled Addie closer. "Stay away from this baby."

His eyes narrowed. "You don't know what you're getting into, lady."

"You're a monster."

"I'll show you a monster if you don't hand over the girl."

"No," she repeated.

"Have it your way." He raised his gun toward Macy's chest.

Gunfire blasted through the air. Macy braced herself for the pain that she was certain would come.

Tanner stood in the doorway and watched the masked gunman collapse to the ground. He hadn't wanted to shoot him, but he'd had no alternative. It was either the man died or Macy.

The choice was a no-brainer.

"Tanner?" Macy whispered.

Macy's stunned eyes met his. In four steps, he reached her, bypassing the gunman, now sprawled on the floor with blood gushing from his chest.

Tanner kicked away the man's gun and quickly checked him for any other weapons. There were none.

He'd already confirmed that the other men he'd shot had fled, so they shouldn't be any danger to Macy or Tanner right now.

Despite all their past history, Macy fell into his arms, her limbs trembling and her eyes watery. The intensity of the moment had broken down their walls...at least temporarily. That situation would have shaken up the strongest of persons.

Tanner had seen it in her eyes: Macy had thought she was going to die.

He'd also seen her willingness to lose her life rather than give up Addie. It was admirable, but not surprising. Macy had always been unselfish.

That was part of the reason why their breakup had been so difficult and hard to accept. So much about it still didn't make sense.

He held her another moment, relishing her familiar, clean scent. She still wore that perfume that smelled like fresh cotton. He'd missed it.

Protect your heart, he reminded himself.

Almost as if she could sense his thought—or as if she'd come to her senses—Macy stiffened in his arms.

Addie's cry turned into a wail, and they both stepped back. Macy drew in a deep breath and raised her chin, obviously trying to compose herself. Addie's chubby fingers reached for Macy's hair, her fingers tangling with the dark brown locks.

Tanner knew that Macy hadn't intended on touching him or letting him hold her. He could still read her like a book, even after all these years. The way she averted her gaze, looked away, rolled her shoulders back.

He had to admit that it had felt good to have her in his arms again. Her hair, as she'd nestled under his chin, had felt soft, and she still fit so perfectly into his embrace.

But it was all over now. There was no need to yearn for the past—not when it could never be re-created.

"Are you okay?" he asked softly, keeping a hand on her arm to steady her.

She nodded, bouncing Addie on her hip, but her trembling limbs belied the action.

"I'm fine." She blanched when she saw his arm.

He looked down. Blood gushed from his biceps. It was only a surface wound, one that looked worse than it actually was. His adrenaline had been pumping so hard that he hadn't noticed the injury.

"You're hurt."

He shrugged. "I've been through worse."

"What happened?"

"Bullet."

Macy squeezed her eyes shut, as if she couldn't stomach the thought of it. When she pulled her eyes open again, her gaze drifted downward to the man on the floor. "Is he...dead?"

Tanner squatted and felt for a pulse on the man's beefy neck. "Not yet, but almost."

She paled even more. "Who were they?"

"I don't know. There's a lot we don't know and a lot that doesn't make sense." He reached down and pulled the man's mask off, anxious to see the concealed face.

A Caucasian man, late twenties, short blond hair and a scar across his cheek stared back at him. Tanner had never seen the man before.

"You know him?" Tanner asked.

Macy shook her head and then looked away.

Tanner felt in the man's pocket. There was no ID. He hadn't expected to find any, but he had to at least try. Maybe they'd get a match off his fingerprints.

The man moaned on the ground, beginning to stir slightly. Tanner knew that trying to talk to him would be useless. If the man came out of this alive, they'd interrogate him until he gave up all the information they needed. But right now he was useless.

"Come on. Let's get you out of this room." He

took Macy's arm, knowing the emotional effects caused by seeing a wounded man. He didn't want to put either Macy or Addie through it.

They stepped into the waiting room, but it also looked like a war zone. Windows were broken. Furniture was overturned. Pieces of drywall littered the floor. Water trickled from the broken edges of the aquarium.

There was also that trail of blood, left by at least one of the men Tanner had shot. They were long gone now. Law enforcement would search for them, but most likely they'd had a getaway vehicle waiting outside.

The way those men had fired showed they were professionals. Maybe former military. Either way, they were skilled. No doubt that they'd thought through their escape plan in case things went wrong.

And things had gone wrong for them—thankfully.

Macy pulled Addie closer, hugging the innocent baby to her.

"Backup should be here any time now," Tanner said, glass crunching beneath his feet.

As the last word left his mouth, a siren sounded outside. He pulled Macy into the corner, desperate to ensure her safety. A moment later, EMTs rushed inside, along with his backup team.

Rick Saul, his boss, hurried toward him. "Tanner, you okay?"

"Yeah, I'm fine. How about Frank? We saw him go down."

"EMTs are evaluating him. It doesn't look good, though." Saul's gaze flickered toward Macy and Addie, and he nodded at them.

Saul was like a rock: emotionless, immovable and strong. He was nearly bald, but had a salt-and-pepper beard, and icy blue eyes. He was a good man, and he'd never let Tanner down before.

"There were at least two gunmen who got away," Tanner said. "They went through the back door, and I can only assume a car was waiting for them there."

"The police are on the lookout for any suspicious-looking vehicles now," Saul said. "There was a camera outside, and we're hoping to find some video footage. There are tire marks by the back door that we can assume belong to the gunmen. We'll do everything we can to locate them."

Tanner wasn't sure why, but he felt certain these guys wouldn't be found. And that would be a shame. At this point, the only way of knowing who sent them was to bring those guys in or get the guy in the other room talking. Because it was obvious these were hired guns someone had sent.

"That baby is the key in all of this," Saul said. "We need to figure out why before anyone else is hurt."

"I agree."

The EMT wheeled the gunman away, two FBI agents flanking either side of him.

Tanner turned to Macy. "We need to get you out of here and to a more secure location."

"But—" she started.

He squeezed her arm again, desperate to get through to her. "It's becoming obvious that nowhere is really safe. The sooner you're tucked away out of sight, the better."

"Me? Why me? I'm not a part of this."

"You are now."

Her walls came down a moment, and he could see the fear on her face. But when she blinked, she'd plastered on that self-assured image again, the one that made it seem like she was in total control.

The realization squeezed his gut. When he'd known her before, she'd reserved that façade for strangers. But never him. She'd let him see the rawest parts of herself.

This was just another reminder of how things had changed.

Tanner led her toward the door.

"You're coming too, right?" she asked.

He nodded. "Yes, I am."

"But you're bleeding."

"I can have an agent stitch me up once we're somewhere safe."

"Are you sure?"

"It's just a surface wound. I'll be fine."

Before they reached the door, Tanner looked at the ground and frowned.

A picture of Macy that had once been hanging on the wall now lay on the ground. The glass was shattered, and two bullet casings rested atop it.

He swallowed hard. That wasn't a sign of things to come.

He would make sure of that.

THREE

Everything happened in a whirlwind. One minute, Macy was waiting for a client, the next moment, she was whisked inside an FBI sedan, secure and snug in the back seat with Addie screaming beside her in a car seat.

If only she could cradle the child. Give her a warm bottle. Change her diaper.

She could do none of that right now.

Macy hadn't had time to ask questions or process anything. Not really. Too much was happening all at once, with little time to breathe even.

Just then, Tanner hopped into the back seat beside her. He tapped the seat in front of him, and the driver—Special Agent Williams, as he'd been introduced—took off.

Macy tried to ignore just how close Tanner was to her. She wished she couldn't smell his leathery scent. She wished any other FBI agent had shown up at her door today, for that matter.

But no, it had to be Tanner. Her life insisted on coming back full circle.

Addie wrapped her tiny hand around Macy's finger, and Macy murmured in an attempt to soothe her. She whimpered then cried then tapered the sound into another whimper.

Meanwhile, Tanner spoke to Agent Williams in the front seat, their mishmash of words barely discernible to Macy as Addie continued to wail.

All Macy cared about right now was getting away and keeping this child safe.

Her gut clenched as she replayed each moment in her mind. She remembered the cold fear that had trickled inside her. The battle-heavy smell of ammunition. Each heart-pounding second that had ticked past at a painstaking pace. They were all stark reminders that death could show up at a moment's notice.

Her day had started so normally yet had turned into this one with an edged desperation.

Addie quieted for a moment, and Macy released her breath as the city landscape blurred past. Maybe she could finally think clearly. She just needed a few minutes of quiet.

She tried to sort her thoughts, but it felt impossible. Instead, she watched the road as they turned off the highway and onto a more rural street.

Talk to Tanner. Find out what's going on.

As she opened her mouth, she noticed him

look over his shoulder. His facial muscles tightened, and the air around her changed from semi-relaxed to super charged. She felt the subtle shift.

Tanner exchanged a look with Agent Williams in the rearview mirror. Williams gave a barely perceptible nod to Tanner before speeding up.

Something was going on.

"Tanner?" Her voice came out like a croak. She tried to keep calm, fearing that Addie might sense any unease and begin wailing again.

"It's nothing to worry about."

"What's nothing to be worried about?" she rushed. "Are we being followed?"

The thought startled her. She glanced behind her and saw a black sedan with tinted windows there. How long had it been there? And why was the driver following so closely?

Before Tanner could answer her question, the sedan suddenly sped until it was right on their bumper. Agent Williams pressed the accelerator, and they charged down the highway, easily topping ninety miles an hour.

Macy closed her eyes and lifted a prayer. *Dear Father, protect us. Protect Addie. Please. This baby doesn't deserve this.*

"Hold on!" Tanner drew his gun from his shoulder holster and looked out the back window.

Macy had hoped the danger had passed and the worst was over. This was only getting more dangerous by the moment.

Macy flung her arm over Addie's car seat, determined to use as much of her body as possible to cover and protect the baby from whatever danger might come.

As if Addie sensed what was happening, she let out a whimper that quickly turned into a wail. Macy had been able to protect her from the danger earlier, but as peril surrounded them once again, no amounts of smiles or baby talk could reassure the child right.

Agent Williams made a sharp turn onto a side road.

There were fewer people to get hurt here, she realized. Fewer casualties if things turned ugly during this car chase.

And things were most likely going to turn ugly.

Macy wanted to glance behind her, but she couldn't. She could hardly breathe, hardly remain calm. People always said she could keep her head in emergencies. Right now, panic was desperately trying to claw its way to the surface.

Just then, the car lurched.

The other driver had run into them. Was he trying to run them off the road?

Anger burned inside her. How could someone put a child's life in danger like this? Why were they going to such extreme lengths?

The car swerved again, followed by the sickening sound of metal crunching into metal.

"Hold on!" Tanner yelled.

He put his window down and snaked his body through the opening until his hips rested on the door. He angled himself toward the other car and pulled out his gun.

The blood drained from Macy's face. Tanner was going to get himself killed!

Macy prayed even more fervently and crouched down farther over Addie. She didn't know what was going to play out over the next several minutes. She wasn't sure she wanted to find out, yet she had no choice.

A pop sounded.

Tanner had fired his gun. Her ears rang at the sound, fading to a dull hum. Addie screamed.

She glanced behind her. The car behind them turned abruptly, brakes squealing uncontrollably as the driver tried to right the vehicle.

Tanner ducked back inside.

But just as he did, there was another pop.

Their own vehicle began to veer all over the road. Their tire must have been shot out. It was the only thing that made sense.

As the car careened into a ditch, Macy was pulled forward. She closed her eyes and prayed harder than she ever had before.

Tanner gave his head a moment to right itself as the car jerked to a stop with a sickening thud. They'd crashed into the ditch and now the engine hissed, as if angry about it. Smoke escaped from the hood. Otherwise, things were strangely silent.

He glanced at Macy and Addie. Both looked dazed but fine. Addie screeched, but the sound let Tanner know that she was alive and well enough to object to the situation. That had to be a good sign.

"Are you okay?" He touched Macy's shoulder, trying to pull her out of shock.

She flinched at his touch but nodded stiffly. "I… I think so."

"Addie?" He needed to confirm his initial thought.

She glanced down and nodded again. "She's as mad as a hornet, but she doesn't appear injured."

Tanner's gaze shot forward. Shawn—Agent Williams—slumped over the steering wheel, and blood trickled from his forehead.

"Shawn," he muttered, reaching forward.

The agent didn't respond. Tanner put a hand to his neck. His pulse throbbed there. *Thank God. No more injuries. Please.*

Quickly, Tanner grabbed the phone from his pocket and called for backup. As he did so, he looked behind him in time to see the other driver dart from his car. Tanner had managed to shoot out his front tire, and now that car wasn't drivable.

The bad guy would try to either escape on foot

or would continue his mission of trying to hurt them from the safety of the woods.

Tanner knew that the danger was far from being over. He had to protect Addie and Macy, whatever the cost. The whole scenario went much deeper than he could have ever guessed.

He grabbed Addie's carrier. The baby was safer in her seat than she would be without the added protection it offered.

"Come on!" he told Macy. "Use the car as a shield."

She scrambled from the back seat and joined him outside. Tanner tugged her to the ground and pulled out his gun.

The woods across the street. That was where the other driver had run. Tanner had a feeling the man would make another grab for Addie and was simply gathering his wits right now. He had to stay a step ahead of him.

"How about Agent Williams?" Macy asked, her breathing more shallow than it should be. "Should we get him out?"

Tanner glanced at Shawn Williams as he slumped against the steering wheel. To try and get him out now would put his life in danger. Tanner needed to be alive in order to protect Addie and Macy.

Instead, he opened the passenger door and released Shawn's seat belt. The agent slumped into the passenger seat.

Out of sight from a potential shooter.

Just as the thought entered Tanner's mind, one of the windows shattered. Another bullet had exploded across the air.

"Give it up!" Tanner yelled, gripping his gun and remaining behind the car. "This isn't going to the end the way you want."

Silence answered back.

There must have been someone else at the psychotherapy center. Someone who'd been waiting outside and had followed Tanner and Macy when they'd fled. Maybe this had all been a part of their plan.

He briefly glanced down. Macy was huddled near the sedan. She rocked Addie back and forth in her car seat. The baby's eyes were as wide as saucers and watery. She was fighting tears. Fighting wails.

Thank goodness Macy was here to help him with the baby. He wouldn't be able to handle all of this on his own. Despite the hard feelings between the two of them now, they'd always been a good team. They'd even been able to finish each other's sentences at one time. They'd been that in tune.

Another bullet smashed the stillness around them.

Addie let out a loud wail at the noise, and Macy began trying to shush her, speaking in gentle, calming tones to the baby.

Tanner had to see if he could spot the shooter. He could tell from the bullet trajectory in what general direction the man was located. But that didn't mean he was standing still in one spot.

Tanner rose ever so slightly and scanned the woods.

There!

The barrel of a gun reflected in the sun.

Tanner aimed and took a shot.

Someone yelped.

He'd been hit! Tanner's aim had found the shooter.

Addie screamed more adamantly at the loud noise.

"Macy, stay here," he instructed. "And stay down."

This was his chance to catch the man—provided he was still alive. And Tanner hoped he was. If he could question the man, maybe they would obtain some answers and get to the bottom of this.

Macy nodded, fear drawn in the depths of her eyes. But he could see the strength there also. "I've got this."

With that last assurance, he took off in a run toward the woods. He reached the tree where he'd last seen the man. He was gone. But a faint trail of blood stretched across the ground, along with some subtle boot prints.

Careful to remain shielded and on guard, Tanner followed the tracks through the woods.

How much farther could the man make it? He was losing a significant amount of blood. Certainly, he'd pass out soon, when his adrenaline wore off.

Tanner paused and listened. Was that a twig breaking?

He crept forward, still bracing himself for whatever may come.

Just as he took another step, a man burst from the underbrush ahead. He darted away from Tanner.

Tanner raised his gun, but the man wove between trees. There was no way he could shoot him. Besides, he didn't want to kill the man. He needed to capture him.

He took off after him instead.

Just as he reached a clearing, the man dove into a waiting car, and they squealed away.

Another car? Had the man called for backup? He must have.

This was a bigger, more elaborate operation than Tanner had guessed. Multiple gunmen. More than one vehicle. An intricate plan.

Then another thought hit him like a slap in the face.

What if these guys turned around and went back to Macy and Addie? They were alone right now. Alone and vulnerable.

He couldn't let anything happen to them. He should have never left them alone, but he'd never imagined a second vehicle.

He couldn't risk making any more assumptions.

He darted back toward them and prayed they were okay.

As he reached the highway, he spotted the empty FBI sedan. Blood rushed to his ears.

Please, let them be okay.

He jetted around the car and froze.

Macy and Addie were still there, huddled at the side of the car.

They were safe…for now. That was all he could guarantee because this whole situation was becoming more and more dangerous by the moment.

FOUR

Two hours later, Macy, Tanner and Addie pulled up to a house in the middle of the Texas country-side. It may have only been an hour from Macy's suburban Houston home, but it felt like a foreign land. And Macy felt like an uninvited guest who didn't belong here.

Everything still felt hazy, like a dream. A nightmare, for that matter.

The FBI had arrived at the roadside scene. They'd questioned her. Tanner had come back from the woods without the shooter, who'd ap-parently gotten away. Agent Williams had been taken away in an ambulance. He was still breath-ing and, from what Macy gathered, they thought he would be okay.

Meanwhile, Addie had cried. Longing for her mom, maybe? Hungry? Tired? Scared?

Tanner got them all moved in to the safe house. There was already a crib set up there and numerous baby supplies. Two other agents stood guard, one at each door.

Once they were settled, Tanner had left again. Macy wasn't sure where he'd gone, but she guessed that he had to debrief with other agents—maybe even a taskforce—about everything that had happened. Plus, his biceps had been bleeding, and he needed to have that checked out.

At the moment, Macy sat on a leather couch in the midsize, rustic cabin. From what she could gather, the place had three bedrooms upstairs and an all-encompassing great room downstairs. Wood planks comprised the walls, and mounted deer heads and stuffed bears were the accessories of choice.

Addie had drifted to sleep in her arms after a bottle, and Macy knew she should put the baby down, but she couldn't. She needed to hold her and know she was okay. She wished she worked with babies this young. The instant bond she felt with Addie did something strange to her heart. It captured it, melted it and twisted it in knots, all at the same time.

This poor, poor baby. A child should never be in the middle of something like this. Whatever *this* was.

In the quiet, Macy tried to let everything sink in.

Was all of this really happening? It seemed

surreal. Confusing. Overwhelming. Who were those men? Who was the baby? There was one thing she was certain of: that man would have killed her if Tanner hadn't come when he did.

Macy shivered at the thought.

She glanced at her watch. She should be headed out to Bible study right now. She was supposed to lead a discussion on the women of the Old Testament. Ruth was tonight's topic.

What would everyone think when she didn't show up? Honestly, it didn't really matter. All that mattered was keeping this sweet baby safe.

The agent standing near the door put his phone to his ear and muttered something Macy couldn't understand. The next instant, tires crunched on gravel outside.

Her pulse sped. Was it Tanner? Or was it the bad guys? Had they been found?

She watched the door, her nerves feeling ragged.

She held her breath, only releasing it when the door opened and… Tanner stood there.

Just as had happened earlier, excitement buzzed up her spine. He was still so handsome and so sure of himself, from his dimples all the way down to those dusty cowboy boots. His outer attributes had only been part of the reason why she'd been so attracted to him.

Though he was as tough as nails on the outside, he also had a soft heart for those he cared about, and he would have bent over backward for her. And that had been part of their problem.

His eyes locked on her, and he sauntered across the room. He paused in front of her and knelt until they were eye to eye.

"I'm sorry, Macy." He kept his voice low as he glanced at Addie.

She pulled her gaze up to meet Tanner's. Looking at Addie was safer.

He still looked as strong and sure as ever, but worry had crept into his gaze. She also saw it in the tautness of his shoulders and in the grim lines at his forehead.

For a moment—and just a moment—Macy wished she could do something to relieve his worry. No words would do it, but the man needed someone to give him a hug or make him some coffee. But nurturer was no longer her role.

"Sorry for what?" She cleared her throat and tried to forget the image of wrapping her arms around him. Of feeling his strong, protective embrace.

"I didn't mean to involve you further than coming to your office today to ask if you would help identify Addie or her mother. But now, whoever is behind this has already seen you and probably thinks you're involved."

Her throat constricted. "What's that mean?"

Apology stretched through his gaze. "It means

now you're part of this, whether you wanted to be or not."

"Are you serious?" Certainly he wasn't. In her mind, the FBI would question her. She'd look through her files, sharing any pertinent information with them. And then she'd go home and return to her normal life.

"Unfortunately, I am. These guys know who you are, where you work. I'm afraid you're also a target now."

Macy leaned back into the couch cushion, the steady sound of Addie's breathing and the warmth of the baby's body soothing her a moment. "What is going on here? This is bigger than a custody dispute, which was my first assumption when you came to me."

"We honestly have no idea at this point. Based on what happened at the therapy center today, we know without a doubt that the stakes are high." He drew in a deep breath. "The choices you have at this point are: you stay in protective custody alone, or you stay in protective custody with Addie. I know what I hope you'll do, but it's your choice."

Macy glanced down at the sweet sleeping baby, and her stomach lurched with protectiveness for the child.

Leave Addie? Macy couldn't fathom doing that at this point. She and the baby had bonded quickly. But, on the other hand, this was her one chance to get away from Tanner and distance herself from him. But she had other questions first.

"Why me, Tanner? Why did Addie's mom scribble *my* name on that piece of paper?"

He stood and lowered himself beside her on the couch, stretching his legs out. "We're trying to figure that out."

Macy tried not to get distracted by his closeness, by the warmth exuding from his body. "But you think I could be connected to this case somehow."

He nodded slowly. "It's a possibility."

The thought of that made her head spin.

She made a quick decision. "Of course I'll stay here and help. Addie needs as many advocates as she can get." She shivered. "This all just seems so horrible."

"I agree. We all do. We're going to track down the person behind this. But, until then, it's like you said—we have to watch out for the best interests of the child."

"It's good to have people who are worried about you," she finally said. "Who will stand beside you no matter what."

Tanner's gaze studied hers another moment before he nodded, a flash of something painful in his gaze. "It does."

She didn't bother to expend the mental energy to figure out what he was thinking. Instead, she did what she did best. She planned. Thought everything through. Developed a plan of action. "I have no clothes except what I have on."

"We'll get you some. Toiletries, as well. Just make a list."

She swallowed hard. "And we'll stay here until this…this…blows over?"

She made it sound like a misunderstanding when it was so much more. And she knew that but didn't know how to follow up on her words without making things even more awkward.

"That's correct."

His grim tone only drove home how serious this situation was. "I'm scared, Tanner."

"I'm not going to let anyone get to you, Macy. I promise."

She believed him. It may have been the most unwise decision Macy could have made, but deep inside she knew Tanner would die rather than let her be harmed.

She cleared her throat, unable to handle her thoughts. "I should call my assistant. She'll need to cancel all my appointments—"

"Macy—"

She couldn't stop now. All she had were her thoughts to contend with, all that she could truly control in this rapidly deteriorating situation. She wanted to believe she wasn't totally helpless. "Of course, she won't be able to get to the calendar until the office opens back up again." The words caught in her throat.

The office would never be the same. Not after the violence that had taken place there today. A therapy center was supposed to be a place for peace and healing. All of that had been shattered, though.

"It will all get taken care of," Tanner assured her. "If you do call her, you'll have to use the phone we give you."

She froze. "You think my cell is being tracked?"

"It's a risk we can't take."

She took the phone Tanner handed her and nodded.

"You can't tell anyone where we are, either," Tanner said. "You understand that, right? One wrong move, and there will be more people hurt."

Her blood chilled. No more trauma. No more people suffering at the hands of evil men.

Just then, Tanner's phone rang. He put it to his ear and muttered something into the mouth piece. When he hung up, he turned to her.

Something else was wrong, Macy realized.

"Tanner?"

He pulled his gaze to meet hers. "My partner—the one who was at Third Day with me—just died. This is no longer about stopping people from getting hurt. It's about stopping anyone else from dying."

* * *

Tanner paced the safe house's living room, trying to sort out his thoughts. Mourning the loss of his friend. Wondering how the man's family was taking the news.

He'd call later and show his respects. He still couldn't believe that Frank was gone, though. It only fueled his desire to get to the bottom of this. Addie needed protection. Frank and his family needed justice.

As nighttime fell and some of the shock wore off, the residents of the house had nibbled on some food that one of the agents had brought. It was just some fresh fruit and bagels, but it would do. No one seemed to be especially hungry right now.

Tanner continued to pace and mentally reviewed all the precautions that needed to be in place to ensure Macy and Addie's well-being here at the safe house.

One agent was stationed at each door. And with Tanner there as well, it meant three men, for one baby—and one beautiful woman.

The years between them had only made Macy look more appealing. He hadn't thought that was possible. To Tanner she'd always been knock-him-over gorgeous. Easily the most good-looking woman in the room—and one of the most humble as well.

Seeing her with Addie in her arms brought

back images of what had once been his dreams of a future with Macy. Those dreams had died a quick and painful death.

He'd assumed their paths would never cross again, given he was in law enforcement and she'd moved to a new state and worked as a psychologist. Their ties had been severed.

Until now.

But sitting next to her on the couch, smelling the sweet aroma of her perfume, and seeing those flecks of emotions in her eyes had taken him back in time. Taken him back to when they'd been in love. When she'd offered hopeful grins and gentle touches and the promise of forever.

He shoved those thoughts aside.

The only thing he needed to think about was this assignment.

Saul had made it clear that this investigation was their first priority. Tanner wasn't usually in the bodyguard business, but he'd do whatever necessary to see this through to completion.

This was just the most bizarre case he'd ever encountered. And it had him more on edge than almost any other investigation he'd worked before. What was going on with baby Addie? Was she a part of a baby smuggling ring?

If so, did smugglers really go so far as to send trained gunmen to kidnap babies? Did they really kill people just to sell a child on the black market? It seemed so unlikely.

Yet what other reason could there be for Addie to be such a commodity?

Macy had mentioned a custody dispute. The actions of the last day would be extreme, even in that scenario.

So what else did this leave?

"I'm sorry about your partner." Macy's voice pulled him from his thoughts.

"Thank you."

She continued to observe him from her seat on the couch. "You're nervous."

He paused and realized that even though there was a crossword puzzle on her lap, her attention had been on him. She'd always been a watcher this way, perfectly content to stand back and observe life going on around her. It wasn't that she didn't play an active part. It was just that she liked trying to figure people out.

She could still read him, the same way Tanner could still read her. The fact made him more uncomfortable than he liked to admit. Could Macy see how much she'd hurt him? Could she sense that he hadn't had a serious relationship since then, that his heart still hadn't quite recovered?

You're nervous, she'd said.

He stopped pacing and stood in front of her, unease still jostling inside him. "The stakes are high."

"You didn't get into this position with the FBI by not being great at what you do," Macy said with a frown. "I know you can handle it. It's what you've always lived for."

Was there a touch of bitterness to her voice? Why? She was the one who'd left him without a good explanation. He didn't feel like this was the time or place to address their past. Not when people's lives were on the line.

"Macy, I thought those other agents could handle things today also, and look what happened. I don't want to scare you, and maybe I'm speaking too honestly, but I've always been able to speak my mind with you."

Something flickered through her intelligent brown eyes. "Please do. I prefer the truth."

He took off his hat for just long enough to run a hand through his hair. "Something about all of this just doesn't make sense to me."

She readjusted her legs beneath her. "You can't pinpoint what?"

He shook his head. "Not yet. I can't imagine someone's motive for going through all this trouble, though."

"Can you tell me again about what happened when the baby was dropped off at your office?"

"A woman came by in a cab," Tanner started. "She acted panicked. She told us the baby's name was Addie, and they were both in trouble. She didn't want her baby to be harmed."

"Didn't you try to stop her from leaving?" Macy asked.

"Of course. But she left the baby with a guard outside the parking lot. He didn't have time to do anything except hold the baby and call for help."

Macy nodded thoughtfully. "Why didn't you call Social Services? Isn't that the norm in a case like this?"

"We decided to check everything out first. We didn't want to put an innocent foster family in danger, in case there was any truth in this woman's words."

"I'm surprised the mom didn't leave Addie with someone in her family." She glanced at the baby sleeping in the portable crib in the corner.

"Families aren't always safe places," Tanner said. "Who knows what the mom's history with her own family is?"

"That's true. There are some wounds so deep that even time can't heal them, not matter what we might want to believe."

Was that statement pointed to him? Because she was the one who'd walked away. He tightened his jaw and pushed the thought aside. "You're right. There are things that we'll never move past."

She owed him more than a goodbye letter, especially after everything they'd shared. But she'd left, leaving him with no answers. So he'd poured himself into his work.

Ever since Tanner was a child, he'd wanted to bring justice to bad guys and help those in need.

Taking that away from him would be like taking water from a dehydrated man: he wouldn't survive.

The memories brought a wave of melancholy. This was going to be a long assignment, being here with Macy. Filling his time reliving memories both good and bad. He ran a hand over his face.

Just then, Addie stirred in the corner crib, and Macy went to retrieve her. She picked up the baby and began talking in low tones.

Tanner's gut clenched. She looked like such a natural. He and Macy should have been able to have this kind of life together. Sure, they'd been too young. But they could have made it work— if Macy hadn't decided to walk out and altered their futures forever.

FIVE

The first opportunity Macy had, she'd scurried off to her bedroom. She'd insisted on taking Addie and keeping her crib in her room. She'd given Tanner a terse good-night and then closed the door.

Macy needed time to process, and she needed to be away from Tanner to do so. Just as always, the man sent her emotions into a tailspin. She couldn't handle that right now. She already had enough on her plate without adding a serving of regrets.

She leaned against the door in her room and tried to rein in her thoughts. Why would someone leave her baby at the FBI field office? What did Macy have to do with any of this? Why was her name in the baby's diaper bag?

Macy had never seen Addie before today. She found it hard to believe that she was linked with this in any way, except that she'd been in the wrong place at the wrong time today. Those gunmen had followed Tanner to her office.

But there was one thing Tanner had said that did create a connection—if a minor one. The fingerprints of the man who'd been shot in the office matched that of a felon from Oklahoma.

Macy had just moved here from Oklahoma six months ago.

She shook her head. That had to be a coincidence. The man's name and picture hadn't been familiar to her. Tanner might not be as convinced, but he'd remained mostly quiet about any possible connections. Knowing Tanner, he would probably check it out not only during work hours but on his own time. He was that type of guy. He crossed every *t* and dotted every *i*. He wouldn't stop until the job got done and until he got it done right.

Macy moved to the bed and lay down. She pressed her head into her pillow, wishing all her burdened thoughts would disappear. Wishing she could go to sleep, wake up and realize all this was a bad dream.

Finally, after tossing and turning for several hours, Macy couldn't take it anymore. She threw the covers off and decided to get some water—quietly, so she wouldn't disturb anyone.

The entire house seemed incredibly still, as if everyone slumbered, when she stepped into the hallway. The thought was hard to fathom considering everything that had happened. But maybe when you were the FBI, you learned to sleep during unrest or you'd never get shut-eye at all.

Macy reached the first floor and tiptoed toward the kitchen. She gasped when she spotted someone standing in the living room.

It was one of the FBI agents who was staying here.

Of course.

Macy grasped her fluttering heart, and her shoulders sagged with relief. The agent was blond and twentysomething with an honest-looking face. He'd seemed nice enough when they'd spoken earlier.

"Sorry," Macy muttered. "I should have known someone would have night duty. You just startled me."

He remained stiff and on guard. "That wasn't my intention. I'm standing guard while everyone rests."

"I'm going to grab some water," she said, nodding toward the kitchen.

"Help yourself."

"Agent Armstrong, right?" She stepped into the kitchen.

He shrugged. "Just call me George, since we'll be working together closely for a while."

"George, it is." She paused and shifted her weight. "How long have you been with the FBI, George?"

"Only a year. This is my first assignment like this."

"Oh, yeah? Have you worked with Agent Wilson a lot?" She was just trying to make small talk, but suddenly it felt invasive. She wanted to take the question back. Tanner was none of her business.

"Several times. I've never met a more dedicated agent."

His words caused her to think a little too much. "Is that right?"

Armstrong nodded. "Some agents just live for this stuff. He's one of them."

"It's a good thing he's not married, huh?" Her words were tinged with a touch of bitterness.

"I'd say. It's good for the people he works to find justice for, at least. Some agents just aren't cut out for a family."

Macy grabbed a glass from the cabinet and walked to the sink, not wanting to continue this conversation anymore. It just confirmed what she already knew: Tanner wasn't the family type.

She flipped the faucet on and let the clear liquid fill the cup. As she did, her gaze wandered out the window in front of her, and she scanned the black landscape outside.

Darkness stared back at her. Of course. It was

1:00 a.m., and they were in the country. There were no streetlights out here. Not even a full moon tonight.

Suddenly, her muscles jerked with surprise. She blinked, clearing her vision.

There *was* a light in the distance. Two lights. Moving. Bobbing.

Like someone walking through the forest with a flashlight.

Macy dropped the glass into the sink, and it shattered into a thousand tiny shards. She hardly noticed as she slowly backed away from the window. Memories of the earlier attack filled her thoughts. Caused panic to take root inside her.

Had someone followed them here? Would they finish what they had started?

The image of the injured man at the psychotherapy center filled her thoughts. The blood. The near loss of life. The fear that hung heavy in the air.

"George," she whispered. She raised a shaky finger toward the window and continued to back away.

The agent appeared at her side, his hand reaching for the gun at his waist. "What's wrong?"

"Someone's out there," Macy said, her voice trembling and thin.

When would this nightmare end? Macy had thought they were safe. That maybe she could breathe for a moment. That she could take some time to sort her thoughts and gather her wits until this blew over.

It seemed that wasn't going to be happening any time soon.

"What do you mean someone's out there?" He rushed to the window.

"I saw a flashlight in the distance. In the woods. Two of them."

"Are you sure?"

Macy nodded, unable to get the image out of her mind. "Positive."

He pulled out his phone and made a call, suddenly all business. "Move to the center of the room, away from the doors. And stay down."

His voice was marked with a definitive sense of urgency.

Five seconds later, Tanner rushed down the stairs.

He paused by her, and she could feel the adrenaline pumping off him. "Are you okay?"

Macy nodded, unsure if she was okay at all. Her limbs were a trembling mess, and she could hardly breathe as anxiety tried to close in.

"Tell me what you saw, Macy."

She swallowed hard, desperate to compose herself. "It looked like flashlights bobbing in the distance. Like people were out there. Like they followed us here."

"How many?"

"Two."

His jaw flexed, and his gaze narrowed. "We're going to check it out."

She nodded and pointed behind her, wishing her head would stop swirling. "I should keep an eye on Addie."

"Go upstairs. Wait with her. Stay there until we know what's going on. I'll leave Armstrong here to stand guard."

Not this again. The waiting. The anticipating. The wondering. It would be a replay of what had happened earlier at the therapy center.

Her nerves couldn't take it.

Before she hurried up the stairs, Tanner grabbed her arm.

"I'm not going to let anything happen to you or Addie, okay?" His voice left no room for argument or disagreement.

Warmth flushed through her. The reaction was illogical, considering how much Tanner had hurt her. But, for a brief second, she'd believed him. Even appreciated him. And that was something she hadn't felt in a long time. Five years long.

Before Tanner could see the clashing emotions inside her, she rushed upstairs.

She darted into her room and over to the baby. She peered into the portable crib and released her breath. Addie was still sleeping peacefully with a blanket covering her lower half, and her hands thrust high above her head.

Thank you, Lord.

Macy locked the door. She paced, unable to sit still. Unable to stop picturing those lights. Unable to stop thinking about worst-case scenarios about what might happen next.

Against all logic and good sense, she crept toward the window. She had to know what was going on. Remaining in the dark was a hard spot to be in. A spot she didn't *want* to be in.

Careful to remain at the edge of the window, Macy peered through the crack between the curtain and window frame. This room faced the same direction as the kitchen—so she could see the woods behind the house.

But she saw nothing. No lights. No movement.

What did that mean? Had she imagined it? No. She was sure she hadn't.

She clenched her jaw. Preparing herself for anything. Because Macy would fight with every last ounce of her being to keep this baby safe.

Tanner stepped outside and onto the front porch, his gun locked and loaded.

Cool nighttime air surrounded him. It was a typical March night in Texas. All was silent except for some crickets and a light breeze that rustled the leaves. He glanced up. Stars twinkled overhead. The piney scent of the forest drifted up to him.

Had someone managed to follow them here?

Impossible. Tanner and his men had taken every safety precaution possible. They hadn't been trailed.

But what if someone had found them anyway? Tanner didn't see how that was possible, but he couldn't rule it out yet.

He flanked the perimeter of the house. At the edge of the house, he paused and observed the woods surrounding them. He listened.

Agent Kyle Manning was on the other side of the property doing the same. Meanwhile, Agent Armstrong stayed inside to protect Macy and Addie.

Tanner heard nothing. The crickets had gone silent. The breeze had died.

He saw nothing. Not even a squirrel. A bird. All was still.

But Macy wasn't the type to make stuff like this up. She'd always been even-keeled and reliable. If she'd said she saw something, then she had.

Tanner darted toward a tree between the house and the woods, his gun still raised and ready. He listened again.

Nothing.

Was someone lying in wait? Did they want him to think no one was here so they could launch a surprise attack? He wouldn't put it past these guys.

He had to remain on guard.

Just then, something snapped in the distance. "Was that you, Manning?" he said into his mic.

"Not me."

He moved closer toward the woods. He knew that whoever these guys were, they were ruthless. They wouldn't blink an eye at harming someone to get what they wanted. The situation at the therapy center today had been proof of that.

Tanner stared out into the haunted-looking trees in the distance. He couldn't use a flashlight right now because that would be a dead giveaway as to where he was. But without one, it was nearly impossible to see until his eyes adjusted properly to the darkness.

"I'll go to the left," Manning said into his earpiece.

"Be careful. I don't like this." Everything about the situation put his senses on alert. He was used to dealing with major crimes. Serial killings, drug busts, grisly homicides. On paper, this shouldn't be so difficult. It was simply protecting an innocent baby who had been left at the FBI field office. But this felt like his toughest assignment to date.

Maybe it also had to do with the fact that he was trying to keep safe the woman he once loved.

SIX

Tanner traveled deeper into the woods, looking and listening for any sign that someone was out here. But all was silent.

Finally, after searching for two hours, he and Manning decided to call it a night. If there had been someone out there, he was long gone by now.

"Anything?" Armstrong asked, meeting them at the door he'd been left to guard.

Tanner shook his head. "Not a thing. You?"

"No, I didn't see anything out there. Maybe Ms. Mills was seeing things."

"She's not the type," Tanner said, his hands going to his hips.

Armstrong stared at him, looking like he'd lost his mind.

"She's not," Tanner said. "She doesn't make things up. Maybe we scared whoever was out there away. We're going to need everyone on duty tonight just in case"

Tanner headed upstairs, taking the steps by two. He had to make sure Addie and Macy were okay and no one had slipped past them.

He remembered that second doorway into the office where he'd stashed Macy and Addie at the therapy center. He grimaced. He wouldn't let that happen again. He wouldn't naively believe that someone was safe when they weren't.

He knocked softly at the door. "Macy, it's me. Tanner."

A split second later, the door opened and a breathless Macy stood there. She wore her black leggings and an oversize shirt. She still looked like she could be in college, especially with her dark hair hanging loose over her shoulders. It was a contrast to the well-put-together look she had at the office. Something about her now screamed innocent and vulnerable.

It took every ounce of his self-restraint not to pull her into his arms and try to offer just a touch of comfort and reassurance. He hated that scared look in her eyes.

The last time he'd seen it…he pushed the memories away. He couldn't go back in time. He couldn't relive those hard, impossible days. He didn't want to.

The beautiful woman in front of him was the same one who'd crushed his heart and altered his plans for the future in a way he hadn't seen coming.

When Macy raised her chin, he saw her inner strength again. "Well?"

He shook his head and leaned in the doorway. "We couldn't find anyone."

She hung her head and squeezed the skin between her eyes. "I saw something out there, Tanner."

"How many lights did you see?"

"Two. At least two." She released a long breath. "What if someone followed us here?"

"I don't see how they could do that, Macy." He kept his voice low in order to not wake up Addie. "But it's a possibility we'll explore. Nothing is off the table at this point."

She rubbed her arms as if she were chilly, but Tanner would venture to guess her chill had come from deep within.

"Do we stay here?" She drew her gaze up to meet his.

Again, the vulnerable look in her eyes made Tanner feel off balance for a minute.

Why did this assignment have to involve Macy? Maybe the good Lord wanted them to finally have some closure. That was the way Tanner was going to have to look at this because nothing else made sense.

"We have to figure that out. As of now, Armstrong, Manning and I are pulling an all-nighter. If anyone comes up to this house, we'll know."

"I'm scared, Tanner."

He broke his resolve and reached forward to squeeze her arm. "Anyone would be."

She relaxed—but only for a moment—and then she pulled back. She made it look like she had to find her footing. But Tanner knew the truth. She didn't welcome his touch.

He'd been expecting the rejection, but it still hurt in a way it shouldn't. He needed to be more careful and guard himself more closely in the coming days.

Macy cleared her throat. "What now?"

"You get some rest. We'll handle the rest of this."

"I'm not really good at letting other people take care of my problems."

"But these aren't really your problems. Unfortunately, we pulled you into them."

"So now they *are* my problems. These guys know who I am. They've destroyed my workplace and turned my life upside down. I'd say I'm involved."

He released a breath. He'd had no clue any of this would happen when he stopped by to see Macy today. Things had unfolded quickly. Dangerously.

"You're right," he said. "And I'm sorry. I wish you weren't in the middle of this. I really do."

"Of course you couldn't have known," she finally said. Just then, Addie began stirring. "I'd better get her a bottle."

Tanner nodded and took a step back. "Yeah, I guess so. We'll talk later."

As soon as the sun began to rise the next morning, Tanner and Armstrong headed outside to search the woods for clues as to what had happened last night. Tanner stepped carefully through the forest, looking for any footprints, fibers, broken branches or trampled underbrush.

The whole property was surrounded by an eight-foot fence. There was a gate near the entrance, which was set off from the house by at least a quarter mile. The cabin wasn't even visible from the street.

To get through the gate, one had to punch in a special code. Tanner would have been alerted via his cell phone if someone had done that.

That only left the possibility of someone climbing the fence. If they'd done that, there most likely would be footprints on the soft ground. It had been down pouring only a day ago, so the soil was still soft. And most likely, there would be tire tracks outside of the fence.

Tanner saw nothing, no proof at all that someone had been in these woods last night. That was both a relief because it meant no one had found them, and it was disturbing because Macy seemed so adamant about what she'd seen.

Macy was already downstairs and feeding Addie a bottle when they got back. Her eyes were warm on Addie, as if she'd already decided it was her personal mission to keep the baby safe. Macy's hair had been pulled back into a ponytail this morning and her face was absent of any makeup.

She looked beautiful. She'd always been beautiful. Though it had been the first thing that had drawn Tanner to her, she was much more than a pretty face. She was intelligent, compassionate, even witty. He'd been proud to have her on his arm and to be able to call her not only a friend but his fiancée.

The sight of Macy with the baby twisted his insides in a way it shouldn't. It stirred up memories of his plan to spend forever with her. Of hopes of forever. Of a future outside of law enforcement and instead with a family.

He quickly shoved those thoughts aside before they turned bitter and churned like bile inside him. He'd wrestled with those feelings for a long time. They'd kept him awake at night. Had infected his thoughts until he built up a wall around himself.

Macy straightened when they walked in. "Well? Did you find anything? Any clues?"

He and Armstrong exchanged a look.

"There's nothing out there." Tanner pulled out a seat across from her at the kitchen table.

She blinked as if she hadn't heard him correctly. "What do you mean?"

"We searched the grounds, looking for any signs that our location had been breached," he said. "There were no footprints, other than our own. There was no evidence that the fence surrounding this place had been climbed. No tire tracks outside of the fence. Nothing."

"But I saw something." Her voice left no room for doubt, and her gaze was unwavering.

"I'm not saying you didn't see anything. I'm only saying we couldn't find any evidence."

"What does that mean? Are we staying here?" She rocked her body back and forth, soothing Addie who was becoming agitated as she finished her bottle.

"It's far riskier to try and move again. We're more likely to be spotted."

She frowned and leaned back, her gaze clouding. "So, you don't believe me. Because if you did, we'd be out of here."

He tried to keep his defensiveness at bay. "It's not that simple. I believe that you believe you saw something."

She looked away, her jaw locking. "I understand."

She clearly didn't understand and seemed to somehow take it personally that they'd found no evidence. She'd always been stubborn once she set her mind to something.

But Tanner's job wasn't to convince her. She wasn't even supposed to be here. He wasn't supposed to be in charge of watching a baby, for that matter. How all of this had fallen into his lap was unreal. Maybe God was trying to teach him some kind of cosmic lesson. He had to face his past hurts and failures head-on.

Tanner stood, hard feelings threatening to rise in him again.

"The security cameras will be set up today," he told her. "Unfortunately, events happened so rapidly that we didn't have surveillance in place last night. Being here is the safest thing we can do right now. At least, until we figure out who these guys are."

"Okay. You know best."

Was there bitterness in her words? He wasn't sure, but he thought he heard a hint of that. He ignored it, knowing they had more important subjects to deal with. They'd been pleasantly polite to each other at first. But was all of that wearing off now? Would their true feelings start to emerge?

Before he walked away, he had one more question. "Did you think of anything else last night, Macy? Anything that would link this baby with you? Maybe someone in Oklahoma?"

She shook her head and shifted Addie to her shoulder to burp her. "No, I still have no idea. There's no one."

He felt the urge to say more, to push her to think more deeply.

Before he could, his phone rang. Saul's name appeared on the screen. He excused himself to step away and take the call.

"We've got some news for you," Saul said.

Tanner paused by the window, staring outside and wondering just what Macy had seen last night. "What's going on?"

"The taxi driver who brought the baby's mom to the FBI headquarters?"

"You found him?" His pulse spiked. Maybe they finally had a lead.

"We did. But he's dead. It looks like someone shot him."

It looks like someone shot him.

Macy replayed Tanner's words as he'd joined her at the table and shared what Saul had told him.

How many more would die before this ended?

She glanced down at Addie. And why was this precious little baby in the middle of this? She rested Addie across her chest, head over her shoulder, and patted her back.

Addie had been fussy this morning. Macy was worried about the baby's ear. Addie kept tugging on it, and Macy knew she needed to keep an eye on her.

Macy's niece had suffered through many ear infections, and Macy wondered if Addie was getting one also. If this continued, she would have to insist on taking her to see a doctor or bringing a doctor here. Macy wouldn't let this baby suffer any more than she already had.

She looked across the room at Tanner as he huddled at the breakfast bar with Armstrong and Manning. A rush of hostility swept through her.

He hadn't believed her when she said she saw lights outside. That hurt way more than she thought it would. Then again, Tanner lived for this job and nothing else mattered to him. Certainly she hadn't.

Macy fought a rush of tears—which was ridiculous. She was a professional woman. She was over this.

Yet Macy had thought she had something special with Tanner. She'd dated since then. But no one measured up to Tanner and the connection they'd shared.

And that was a problem because she and Tanner could never be together.

Macy was a psychologist. She'd studied human behavior. And she should have a better handle on this. But, when she was being honest with herself, she'd admit that she didn't have a handle on her emotions around Tanner at all. Just seeing him again had brought back so many old feelings and hurts.

She looked down at Addie's sweet little expression. Big brown eyes stared up at her, those brown curls framing her perfect round face, and chubby hands reached for Macy's hair. She cooed, and a moment of peace came over Macy.

All she'd wanted for so long was to be a mom. To have a family. She'd never wanted to be married to her career. Sure, she was doing important work. But deep inside, having her a husband and children were her true desire.

"We're looking for your mama," she whispered, gently poking the baby's stomach.

Addie smiled in response.

Macy hoped that they might track down Addie's mom through the taxi company. But a bad feeling brewed in her gut after hearing Tanner's news.

If the taxi driver was dead... Macy shook her head. She couldn't go there. She had to stay positive. Nothing had happened to Addie's mom. She was just lying low until all of this passed.

As much as Macy tried to convince herself to believe it, she couldn't.

"I need your help," Tanner said, approaching her with a laptop in his hands.

"Sure thing. What's up?" She shifted Addie to one side of her lap.

"Your boss from Third Day sent over your files. I need you to look through them and see if anyone rings a bell as a potential relative or connection to Addie."

"I can do that. But what about Addie?"

"I'll take her."

Macy quirked an eyebrow. Tanner seemed more comfortable searching for bad guys than he did calming an anxious baby. But if this was what they needed to do, then so be it.

She stood and lifted Addie into Tanner's arms. "She needs a diaper change."

Before Macy could see Tanner's face, she took the computer from him and got busy.

SEVEN

Two hours later, Macy had searched through all the files that had been sent over. Several clients and former clients were close matches. There were mothers with children similar in age to Addie, but ultimately their infants were either boys, or the women were of a different ethnicity. Macy had worked with some of these children's older siblings. For all she knew, Addie could be someone's sister or cousin. The baby could have been adopted. There just wasn't enough information to go on at the moment.

The truth was that none of these families fit. Macy had hoped for answers, but they weren't to be found in these files.

She leaned back in the chair, trying to clear her thoughts. Her body ached from hunching over the computer for hours. She hadn't wanted a break, though. No, what she wanted was to figure out what was going on and how she was connected to this baby. It couldn't have been a coincidence that her name was scribbled on a piece of paper and left in the diaper bag.

Macy's mind wandered to Oklahoma again. Could Addie's mom be connected to Macy through her work there? It was a possibility. But why would someone drive from Oklahoma City all the way to Houston to find Macy? It was a nearly seven hour trip.

Besides, she wasn't close to any of her clients. Most of them didn't even know where she'd moved to. She'd been careful to keep her private life private. Oftentimes, therapy clients felt an unhealthy connection to their psychologists. She'd read case studies about how that could turn ugly. For that reason, Macy had been very careful about what personal information she revealed.

Despite that, she'd asked Tanner to see if he could request copies of her client list. It was an option worth exploring, especially since they had so few leads right now.

Macy leaned back in the chair and rubbed her eyes in exhaustion. Nothing made sense. And now she was in the middle of this mess, trying to claw her way out. She knew she couldn't walk away, not when Addie's life was at stake. Macy was in this, whether she wanted to be or not.

Tanner emerged from the bedroom, where he'd been trying to get Addie to sleep. He strode back into the living room, his cowboy boots clicking against the wooden floor and his hat pulled down low over his eyes. Somehow, the rowdy cowboy look had always fit him—and had always been very attractive to neat and orderly Macy.

In fact, when the two of them had first met, Tanner had been working security for a football game at the college where Macy was attending graduate school. She'd gotten locked out of her car, and Tanner had shown up to help. They'd ended up going for ice cream after his shift ended, and they'd been inseparable after that.

Until they'd broken up, of course. Macy felt like she'd lost a piece of herself that day. Yet their breakup had been her own doing.

Macy studied Tanner for a brief second, but the only thing she really noticed was that his arms were empty. Eventually, the baby's cries had faded, and silence had filled the space.

"Well?" Tanner asked, clunking toward the table and pausing.

Macy pushed her reading glasses up higher on her nose, unreasonable concern ricocheting through her. "Where's Addie?"

"Don't look so worried. I just got her to sleep and put her down." He tilted his head and observed her with a touch of amusement in his eyes.

Macy felt her shoulders slump with relief. "Sorry for the overreaction. I keep expecting the worst, even when it defies logic. It sounds like you've got the touch."

"I don't know about that. Maybe she was just exhausted from crying so much." He pulled up a seat beside her at the table and glanced at the computer. "Did you find anything?"

She shook her head, fighting a sense of defeat. "I was hoping I might, but none of my clients or their families match this baby. I really have no idea who she might be, Tanner."

"You don't think she's connected through your time in Oklahoma?"

"I've thought of that. But if I was close enough to someone that they would track me down here, you'd think I would remember who that client was."

"As you know, memories aren't always reliable."

She shrugged. "True, but I looked through everything and I didn't see any matches. I just hope this baby's mom is okay. Any updates on what happened to the taxi driver?"

Tanner scrubbed a hand across his jaw, all signs of amusement disappearing. "The local police think an old business associate of the man's may have killed him. Apparently, he had some trouble with drugs when he was younger, even though he'd passed every drug test over the past three years."

Macy crossed her arms over her chest and let

that sink in. "So they don't even think his death is connected with Addie? That seems like too much of a coincidence."

"I agree."

Her thoughts raced through what she knew. Certainly there were some answers that could be found in this man's death. "Don't taxi drivers keep logs of where they've gone and who they've picked up? Were you able to trace anything? Did they give you any clues?"

Tanner leaned back and released a long breath. "Addie was left at the FBI office at noon on Monday. This driver—Rafael—picked someone up at a shopping center at ten on the same day. We think it was probably Addie's mom. We have other agents scouring the parking lots in the area, looking for a car that may have belonged to her. We're also checking security footage at those stores."

"It's a start at least."

"We'll take anything we can get at this point."

Another thought had been pressing on her since the details of this case came to light. She hadn't voiced them aloud, but maybe she needed to. She needed to get it off her chest. "The thing I keep coming back to is this: What could have happened to the mother that she would leave her baby behind? I can't imagine how extreme her situation must have been to do something like this."

Macy wrapped her arms more tightly over her chest, suddenly chilled. She couldn't even imagine what the mother might have been going through. Leaving her baby must have been terrifying.

"The woman told the guard at the gate that the baby was safer with us than with her," Tanner said. "She must have known her life was in danger."

But that still didn't make sense to Macy. "Why didn't she try to stay with you?"

Tanner's gaze flickered to hers. Was he impressed by her line of reasoning? She couldn't be sure, but she thought she saw a touch of admiration in his gaze.

Finally, he shrugged. "Good question. I don't know. She must have had her reasons."

Macy continued to think it through. She'd studied the human mind and how it worked, yet there were still cases that perplexed her. She wanted to crack this, to understand what was going on.

Another thought occurred to her. "What if she had a record, Tanner?"

Tanner leaned back and narrowed his eyes. He was tired, she realized. She could see the signs of exhaustion across his face, and she had the sudden urge to fix him a cup of coffee. But not right now. First, they had to finish talking.

"What do you mean?" he asked.

"The only reason I can think of that she would leave her baby and not stay herself was if she feared you wouldn't believe her," Macy said. "What if she has some kind of criminal past? It might give her a natural distrust for law enforcement."

"It's a possibility." Tanner nodded slowly, as if considering the truth in her statement.

"I don't know how these things work, but is it possible to cross-reference women who've been imprisoned in Oklahoma and who had a baby six months ago?"

"It's a start." He shifted, those inquisitive eyes meeting hers again. "You ever done this before?"

"Of course not. Why?" She began straightening the notes on the table that she'd taken while going through those files, not liking how easily she could be mesmerized by Tanner's gaze.

"You're pretty good at it."

"I just like studying how people think." She'd been trying to figure out how Tanner thought for years but had never succeeded. He remained a mystery to her. Or maybe her problem was that she didn't like the conclusions she came to.

There was the Tanner she thought she knew, the Tanner she'd put up on a pedestal. And then there was the Tanner she'd never known had existed, the man who was more like Macy's father than she'd ever like to admit. Someone who was married to his job above all else. Who resented anyone or anything that got in the way of his career goals.

Yep, that was Macy's dad. He couldn't handle the death of his wife—Macy's mom—so he'd let his work as a doctor consume him. He worked long hours, so much so that Macy sometimes went several days without seeing him. Nannies had taken care of her and her sister instead, although her sister was eight years older and had moved out by the time Macy was ten.

"You're doing a good job at evaluating all of this." Tanner drew in a deep breath. "Macy—"

She sensed he was going to say something personal and braced herself.

Before he could, a wail cut through the air.

Addie was awake.

"I'll go get her," Macy said, rushing to her feet.

Tanner looked at the computer, his earlier nostalgia seemingly gone. He looked all business again. And whatever he was able to say was forgotten.

Tanner had volunteered to take the night shift that evening. If he were honest, he would admit it was because he was concerned. On one hand, he wanted to believe that Macy was seeing things and no one had been outside last night. On the other hand, he knew she wasn't the type to overreact.

He had to be sure they were safe. If someone did know where they were, he felt certain they would wait until it was nighttime to plan any type of attack. The darkness added layers of protection and concealment.

The thought had him unnerved. Not because he doubted his abilities. But because too many people had gotten hurt already. There were too many unknowns and uncertainties.

And then there was Macy.

She'd always thrown him off-kilter, and right now was no exception. Even with the years between them, she had the uncanny ability to make him feel like he was walking on clouds just with one single glance.

Which wasn't a good thing. She'd broken his heart when she left him a letter, saying they needed to break up and offering no explanation. He'd deserved more, especially considering they were supposed to get married. His attempts to reach out to her after had been unwelcomed and unsuccessful.

His dreams of spending forever with her had died. He'd had visions of starting a family together, of waking up each morning to see her face. But she'd crushed all his hopes.

Tanner paced the perimeter of the house, peering out the windows, looking for any sign of danger. All he saw was darkness.

As a sound inside the house drew his attention, he instinctively reached for his gun and pivoted.

He released his breath when he saw Macy padding down the stairs. She looked surprisingly awake, evidence that sleep was eluding her also. Another agent had brought her clothes for her unexpected stay, and right now she wore a pair of black leggings and an oversize blue shirt. She looked cozy and warm—until he saw her eyes. They were filled with angst and worry.

"Didn't mean to startle a man with a gun," she said, meeting him in the living room.

"Can't sleep?" He slid his gun back into his holster.

She frowned and pulled her arms across her chest. "I can't get my brain to turn off. I assume everything has been peaceful outside?"

"So far, so good."

Her frown deepened, and she pulled her gaze up to meet his. "I have a bad feeling, Tanner."

"Bad feelings don't always constitute a bad outcome," he reminded her. He didn't want to worry her by sharing that he had a bad feeling also. That was his job, to be concerned for those things.

She let out a long breath and raked a hand through her hair. "I suppose you're right."

Except that her instincts had always been good. Excluding when it came to Tanner. Then she'd been totally wrong. He didn't bring that up now, though.

Instead, he tried to distract her from her heavy thoughts.

"How's your family?" Tanner asked. It was one of the first truly personal things he'd asked about. He would test the waters and see how she reacted.

Macy lowered herself onto the couch and pulled her knees toward her chest. She looked like she was a teenager again. She seemed so vulnerable and young, and that realization stirred up a protective instinct in him.

"My dad is still working at the hospital," she said.

"I thought he'd be looking at retirement by now."

Macy shrugged. "He's cut back his hours some. He got remarried."

"Did he?"

"To a woman in her forties with two children. Ten-and twelve-year-old girls. They're all really sweet."

"I see." Compassion lined his voice. He knew about Macy's issues with her father and wondered if he was being the dad to his stepdaughters that Macy had always wanted him to be for her. It couldn't be easy to see or experience.

Macy drew in a deep breath, still seeming guarded. "And my sister is living about an hour from here. She's still working as a wedding planner. Her boys are six and eight now, and they love baseball. Every weekend I think they're at a different tournament."

"Six and eight? It doesn't seem possible they're that old now."

"I know. It doesn't seem that long ago that we babysat them."

Tanner shook his head. "No, it doesn't. It was my first experience changing a diaper."

Macy smiled. "I remember."

"So do I." His smile faded. "I'm sure your family is happy you moved back."

"Always. And your family?"

"Dad fishes a lot now that he's retired. My mom has decided she wants to enter a half marathon."

Macy smiled. "That's great. They were so kind to me. I've never forgotten that."

"They always liked you."

His words hung in the air. His parents had been just as disappointed in their breakup as he had. She'd claimed a place in their family, a place that had been empty since she'd left.

Just then, a creak outside caught his ear. Tanner froze, his instincts going on alert. He put a finger over his lips.

"Did you hear that?" he whispered.

Macy visibly tensed. "I heard something."

It could have been Armstrong or Manning.

But Tanner had to be certain. Besides, it almost sounded like it came from the porch.

His muscles pulled taut as plausible scenarios flashed through his mind. Had the bad guys found them? Were they watching them now and just waiting to make a move?

"Stay here," he said in a low whisper.

Macy's face paled. She sank back onto the couch but looked anything but relaxed as she sat upright and alert.

Moving slowly and carefully, Tanner peered out the front window. Darkness stared back. He could vaguely make out the outline of some trees and the edge of the porch, but nothing else. He went window by window and did the same check, searching for anything out of place and visible to the human eye.

He didn't see anything.

"It could have been a deer or a raccoon." He took a step toward Macy.

Even as Tanner said the words, he knew that wasn't it. The creak had sounded too heavy, too hidden.

Suddenly, Macy stood. "Do you smell that, Tanner?"

The scent hit him.

Smoke.

There was a fire somewhere. Close.

"Go get Addie," he barked. "Now!"

EIGHT

Macy flew up the steps, urgency nipping at her heels as she raced to get Addie.

Where there was smoke, there was fire. Wasn't that the saying?

Somehow, she instinctively knew that those words were the truth. Whoever had set this fire had done it on purpose. They wanted to push Tanner, Macy and Addie outside. Into harm. Into a trap.

As she climbed higher, she spotted the flames. They licked the edges of the house, already beginning to consume it.

Despite the heat around her, ice formed in her gut at the thought.

She scooped up Addie, hating to wake the infant when she was sleeping so peacefully. As she did, Macy saw the first flicker of orange outside. Alarm raced through her.

She had to move. Fast.

Macy rushed downstairs, where Tanner waited

for her. He grabbed her arm and ushered her toward the door.

"We don't have time to linger outside," he called over his shoulder to the other agents. "The longer we're exposed, the greater the chances are of someone getting hurt. We've got to move. I'll take Macy and Addie. You two stay together."

"We're not going to try and find out who did this?" Manning asked, confusion rippling across his features.

"Whoever started this fire is most likely waiting for us outside. They have the upper hand right now. We don't have time. Addie's safety is the most important thing."

"Got it," Manning said.

Flames licked the walls now, slowly devouring the house. Tanner pulled out his gun and turned toward Macy. "We don't have much time."

"I gathered that."

Macy could hardly breathe. Just then, Addie awoke with a cry. She looked around, her eyes wrinkling with obvious unhappiness at being jostled from her slumber.

The poor baby. She had no idea what was going on. She didn't deserve this.

Tanner kept his arm around her and Addie. If only Macy had time to grab a bottle. A pacifier. Something to make the baby feel better.

But right now, they had more important issues

to focus on. They'd have to deal with crying and concentrate on staying alive.

"Let's do this," Tanner said. His voice held no room for argument. He was in full-fledged cop mode. This stuff was what he lived for. Saving people's lives. Putting the bad guys behind bars.

He opened the door. Flames licked their way inside.

Macy gasped as the edges of the fire felt dangerously close. She pulled Addie tightly to her chest, determined to protect the baby at all costs.

Manning flanked one side of her and Tanner the other. She held her breath as they slipped outside. She waited for bullets to fly. For a burning sensation to reach her skin. For pain.

But there was none. Not yet, at least.

They rushed to the car. Manning ushered Macy and Addie inside while Tanner climbed into the driver's seat.

There was no car seat. There hadn't been time.

Instead, Macy continued to hold Addie close to her chest, trying to shield her from any incoming danger or threats. Addie's wails only tightened Macy's muscles until they felt like they might snap with tension.

Macy lifted a quick prayer.

Please help us. Help me keep my head right now in this situation. To use all those skills that I teach others.

As Tanner started the car, a bullet shattered the window.

Of course. The men were waiting out here. All of this had been a trap. What else did they have up their sleeve? Had Tanner and Macy been lured into the lion's den?

"Hold on!" Tanner yelled.

Macy pulled Addie to her chest, continuing to pray she would stay safe.

Apparently, these guys had been expecting them to run outside but not to the car. They didn't seem to have a vehicle ready to chase them. That was the good news.

Tanner sped away from the flames engulfing the house, out the gate, and pulled onto the country highway outside.

Addie continue to bawl. Macy bounced her in her arms, still holding tight and praying hard. She waited for another bullet. For screeching tires behind them. For signs that the danger was still real and on their heels.

But she heard nothing other than Addie's wails. Macy spoke in soothing tones, trying to calm her down. "It's going to be okay, sweet baby girl," she whispered. "Macy isn't going to let anyone hurt you. I promise."

She had a feeling this was far from over and that keeping that promise might be one of the hardest things she'd ever have to do.

* * *

Thirty minutes later, when Tanner was sure no one was behind them, he pulled over in a parking lot outside a shopping center. It was dark outside—it was 3:00 a.m.—and only a single overhead lamp lit the deserted area. A few cars passed on the highway in the distance, but otherwise the area was quiet.

His phone rang, and he saw it was Manning. Where had the agents gone? They'd split up after leaving the house.

"What's going on?" Tanner asked.

"We're going to circle back around and head back to the house," he said. "We want to know what happened."

"We all do," Tanner said. "I want to know how they found us."

"Are you guys okay?"

He glanced in the rearview mirror. "Yes, we're as well as to be expected. I don't know where we're headed yet, but we'll be in touch."

Tanner hung up and released his breath. He tried to gather his thoughts amidst the chaos that they'd just barely escaped.

How had someone found out where Addie was? How had these guys eluded the cameras and other surveillance in order to set the place on fire? And the most disturbing question was, what if Tanner, Macy and Addie hadn't gotten out in time?

Tanner didn't want to think about it, but he had no other choice. He had to consider all the risks in this situation. That safe house hadn't been at all as secure as it should have been.

He released his breath and glanced behind him.

Addie's sobs had finally quietened, and she slept in Macy's arms. The baby had cried and cried, despite Macy's efforts to calm her. She'd probably dozed off from sheer exhaustion in the end.

He and Macy had no car seat with them. They hadn't had time to grab one. But they couldn't travel like this for long. It wasn't safe for Addie. But getting away from the fire and the bad guys had taken precedence over car safety when they'd fled from the cabin.

"What now?" Macy asked, her voice soft and tired.

"I've got to get in touch with headquarters. We need another safe house. Now."

"How did they find us?" Macy asked, shifting ever so slightly under Addie's weight.

"I don't know. That's a great question." He ran a hand over his face and peered more closely into the back seat. "Are you okay?"

She nodded after a moment of thought. "My nerves are frayed, to say the least."

"We'll get through this."

Macy frowned. "These guys are persistent.

They really want Addie, and it's disturbing the lengths they're willing to go to."

"I know." He bit back. "There's a piece we're missing here, and none of this makes sense without it."

"What do you mean?"

"Why does someone want this baby so badly that they're willing to kill to get her?"

She nodded slowly. "You're right. There is something we're missing."

He ran a hand over his face again. "I need to make a phone call. Sit tight for a few minutes, okay?"

"Okay."

Within minutes, he'd arranged for another safe house location. An agent would check out the place first and ensure that the proper surveillance was set up. They couldn't let this place be compromised, and Saul assured him that would be the case. They'd take every precaution that was necessary.

"Tanner, there's a car pulling into the parking lot." Macy's gaze was focused on a vehicle in the distance. "Could be a coincidence. But…"

Tanner wasn't taking any chances. He put the car in Drive. "We're getting out of here."

As soon as they hurried toward the exit, the other car sped up, coming toward them.

It was definitely the bad guys. How had they found them?

Dear Lord, help me protect this baby. Please. And protect Macy, too. She's just a civilian who shouldn't even be involved in this.

His hands gripped the wheel even tighter. He had to think quickly and use every ounce of his FBI training.

He turned onto the street.

Rule number one: make sure the public isn't harmed. For that reason, he needed to retreat from this little suburban area and find some country roads. There was a better chance of those streets being deserted. He also knew it would be harder to lose the guys on those deserted roads. There would be fewer places to hide.

Tanner glanced in the rearview mirror. The car continued to gain on him.

He tried to make out the face of the person behind the wheel, but he couldn't. It was too dark outside.

The headlights came closer and closer.

The driver was going to rear-end them.

"Hold on," he muttered to Macy.

He knew that whoever these people were, they wanted Addie alive. They wouldn't try to kill them. Only to run them off the road, take the baby and maybe then put a bullet through Tanner and Macy.

He couldn't let that happen.

He pushed the accelerator to the floor and scanned the road in front of them. Thankfully, this area of the road was wooded. That would afford them more places to hide.

It was their only opportunity.

Taking a risk, Tanner made a sharp left turn onto a side street. He'd put just enough distance between himself and the other car that there was a possibility the other driver hadn't seen him turn.

But he couldn't stop now. No, he cut his headlights and kept driving, full speed ahead.

Tanner took the next left also, onto another rural road. He kept speeding ahead, checking the rearview mirror.

There was still no sign of the other driver.

Suddenly, the road came to a dead end at what appeared to be an old, abandoned farm.

Tanner gritted his teeth.

There was only one thing he knew to do. And he hoped it didn't get them killed.

He charged toward the barn. When he reached it, he pulled through the open doorway, into the dark recesses of the old building, and cut the engine. Wasting no time, he hopped out and shut the outbuilding's weathered sliding doors to conceal the vehicle better. Then he waited with his gun drawn.

Macy rubbed Addie's back with steady, soothing circles. *Stay quiet, little girl. Please, stay quiet.* She closed her eyes, praying that they could somehow disappear from these people who were following them.

Tanner opened the back door of the sedan.

"What do we do now? Do we just wait?" Macy whispered, almost as if the people following them could hear.

"We're too exposed if we stay in the car."

Macy's hands trembled as she carried Addie and scrambled from the car. Tanner waited for them and put a hand on her back. The darkness was so intense that it felt heavy. Macy's throat constricted.

Tanner escorted her away from the door and into a stall far away from the entrance. The dusty scent of old straw and hay tingled her noise, but Macy held back her sneeze.

"Stay low," he whispered.

Before she could respond, she heard a scratching sound behind her. She pulled Addie closer.

Just then, eyes glowed in the darkness and someone lunged toward them.

No, not someone. Something.

A cat.

Macy released her breath and let out a soft laugh.

"Just a barn cat," Tanner whispered.

The cat didn't seem to care that it had scared them. Instead, the tabby sashayed into another stall. Macy shook her head, envying the cat's carefree attitude for a minute.

As silence fell between them, another sound hit her ears.

Tires crunching on gravel.

Macy held her breath.

No, no, no...

She peered through one of the cracks in the barn's siding. Her breath caught. The car had pulled down the lane leading to the farm.

Tanner crouched beside her, one hand still on her back and the other gripping his gun. His presence brought her a strange comfort.

Addie let out a loud babble. Macy put a finger over her lips and bounced the baby. She had to keep her panic at bay.

She looked between the boards again and saw the headlights coming toward the barn.

"Do you think they know we came in here?" she whispered.

"The dust has settled," Tanner said. "At this point, the other driver is just guessing."

Macy held her breath as the car stopped.

Dear Lord, help us. Please.

A man stepped out of the vehicle. Macy strained to see him, to identify him. But it was dark. His headlights did illuminate part of the area by the barn, though.

As he walked closer, she strained for a better look. He was tall and thin with dark hair. Probably in his late thirties. Macy had never seen him before.

He started toward the barn when his cell phone rang, and he paused. "I don't know. I lost them."

Silence stretched another moment.

"What?" the man asked, his voice rising. "Are you sure?"

Just then, Addie let out another squeal.

The man froze and glanced at the barn. Had he heard her?

Macy prayed he hadn't. *Please, Lord. Please.*

"Okay, okay," he said. "I get it. Listen, I've got to run. I'll be in touch."

He walked toward the barn.

Tanner pressed his hand down on Macy's back, obviously feeling her nerves.

He'd heard Addie, and now he was going to come and check things out.

The barn door creaked open, sending Macy's nerves into a tailspin. What would they do if he found them?

Tanner was here. He could protect them.

Still, the unknown left her feeling shaky.

She bounced Addie, praying that the child would stay quiet. Just one more baby gurgle would give away their location and put them all in jeopardy. Yet she knew reasoning with an infant was impossible.

Just then, another screech sounded.

Macy's lungs tightened. What was going on?

The sound was followed by a loud meow.

The cat!

The man muttered something beneath his breath. Footsteps sounded. She looked outside again.

He was going back to his car! He'd thought the earlier sound had been the cat.

Thank You, Lord!

A moment later, he climbed in and pulled away.

Macy released the breath she'd been holding.

"He left," she whispered.

Tanner still looked tense. "Yes, he did. We need to wait a few minutes just to make sure this isn't a trap of some sort."

Macy nodded, settling for his words. She sat back and placed Addie on her lap, ready to wait this out—to do whatever was necessary to get out of this alive.

"You remember visiting my granddad's farm?" Tanner asked.

She smiled, surprised by the memory. She hadn't thought about that farm in years. "I sure do. We had a lot of great times there, didn't we?"

"You remember that barn wedding we went to when my cousin got married?"

She smiled again, finding surprising joy in the midst of these unpleasant circumstances. She knew what Tanner was doing. He was trying to distract her, and it was working.

"How could I forget?" she said. "It was the

most beautiful event I'd ever been to, especially with those lights strung overhead and all of those wildflowers." She paused. "How is your grand-dad?"

"He's doing well. My parents keep trying to talk him into moving in with them, telling him the farm is too much to take care of now that he's in his eighties. Of course he doesn't listen."

"Of course. You both have a little of that Wilson stubbornness."

He tilted his head. "Is that what you call it?"

"That's definitely what I call it. It's the Wild West spirit in you."

"You might have some of that same spirit in *you*."

Macy's smile faltered. "I don't know about that."

"I do."

Their gazes held for a minute.

Finally, Tanner stood. "My grandfather is on the verge of losing his farm, however. Taxes have gone up, but his income has gone down. We've all been trying to pool our money together to save the place before back taxes are due."

"I'm sorry to hear that. It would be a real shame."

"I agree." He released a breath. "I think it's safe to leave now. You ready?"

She nodded.

Tanner offered her his hand. Electricity shot through her as their palms touched. She ignored it.

But Macy couldn't deny how her throat tightened as he helped her to her feet.

Not only was Tanner tough, but he was kind. And the sparks between them were obviously still there.

Time might have passed, but it seemed nothing had truly changed.

NINE

Finally, Tanner, Macy and Addie arrived at the new safe house. Tanner should have felt better, but he didn't. Something wasn't fitting into place about this whole situation, and it left him feeling unsettled.

Macy and Addie waited in the car with the doors locked while he checked out the new location. Armstrong and Manning were on their way. They'd left the scene of the fire after Saul had instructed them to meet Tanner here.

Another team had gone in to investigate what had happened at the first location, and it would be a couple of days before they had answers. What Tanner knew for sure was that someone had set the house on fire in hopes of drawing them out. Thankfully, they'd made it to the car and had escaped before things had turned ugly.

But people who were that careful at planning should have snatched them right away. Shot Tanner and Macy and grabbed the baby. Had something gone wrong? Tanner would guess they'd reacted more quickly than the bad guys had accounted for.

This time, too, the safe house was secluded and out in the country. It wasn't a cabin, but more of a modern vacation home with updated amenities and clean lines.

Tanner found that the security cameras were already in place. There was also a fence surrounding the property, as well as a security gate at the entrance. Granted, that hadn't stopped someone last time.

Once he felt confident that the inside was secure, he went outside to the car. His boots crunched across the gravel, and the sun shone down bright over him. Despite the winter day, the air was unseasonably warm and he hoped it was a promise of good things to come.

Before he reached the car, he heard Addie fussing inside. That poor baby. She'd been through so much in her short little life.

He opened the door and saw Macy bouncing Addie in her arms again. It was a familiar sight, and it never failed to warm him. Macy was a nurturer. She should have a houseful of kids. He knew that was the desire of her heart.

"She's not very happy." Macy looked up at him.

"No, she's not." As if in response, Addie let out another cry, her face distorted with irritation.

"I hope she's not getting sick," Macy said with a frown.

"Me, too." Tanner peered at the child, reaching for her hand in an attempt to help calm her. "Does she feel warm?"

"No. Not yet." Macy shook her head and let out a soft breath. "Maybe she just misses her mom."

"We'll get her a bottle and change her. Maybe that will cheer her up."

"Let's hope."

Tanner turned to her once they were inside. "Do you want me to take her for a few minutes and give you a break?"

He could see the exhaustion written all over Macy's features. This had been taxing on her. The endless crying, the stress of being on the run and leaving everything familiar behind. She was holding up surprisingly well, all things considered.

Macy offered a faint smile. "No, that's okay. I'll take care of her. I don't mind. If you could just point me to the nursery."

Tanner led her to the baby's room, and Macy disappeared inside.

Just as she did, his phone rang. It was Saul. Tanner hoped he might have an update.

"We're going to release the baby's picture," his boss announced.

Tanner's back stiffened at his pronouncement.

He hadn't been expecting that. "What? Are you sure that's a good idea?"

"We're going to see who comes forward. Maybe we'll get a decent lead as to who this baby is. Or maybe the bad guy will somehow show his hand."

"It's risky." The more Tanner thought about this plan, the more he disliked it.

"Don't worry," Saul said. "The baby won't come anywhere near this until we're absolutely certain anyone who comes forward is a match and isn't a danger to the child."

"I'm not sure this is a good idea."

"I'm not, either, but we're running out of options here. The danger is escalating, and we don't have any more answers than we did before."

Tanner paced back into the living and away from the nursery door. "When will this be happening?"

"Tonight. We're going to hold a press conference, and we'll see who comes forward."

"These guys wouldn't be very smart if they did come forward. They have to know we're on to them." There seemed to be so many holes in this plan that Tanner didn't see how it would possibly work.

"Most criminals I know aren't very smart.

These guys seem to be relying on their brute strength. Let's see if we can shake them out."

"If you think this is best," Tanner finally conceded.

"Besides, maybe someone who is related to her will come forward and offer some answers about what is going on."

"I hope so." Hope was usually a good thing. But, in this case, Tanner would choose caution.

"Then let's do this. I'll be in touch."

By the time Macy, Addie and Tanner had arrived at the new safe house it was morning. They'd essentially been up all night.

Macy knew time was of the essence in cases like this, but she also knew she needed to rest if she was going to think clearly. That was why when Addie fell asleep, Macy decided to take a nap as well.

She got a good three hours—just enough to help her feel refreshed. When she emerged from her bedroom, Manning and Armstrong had arrived. They each stood guard by the outside doors.

Her gaze searched out Tanner and found him at the kitchen table. He was poring over something on the computer.

He smiled when he looked up and saw her. "You're awake. Do you feel better?"

Macy sighed and sat down at the table across from him. "Maybe a little. I thought I might wake up and realize this was all a dream."

"Unfortunately, it's not." He frowned sympathetically.

"Did I miss anything while I slept?" She yawned, still not fully awake.

Tanner ran a hand over his face, looking exhausted. He obviously hadn't slept any. He'd probably been working the whole time. That sounded like him. A workaholic, sacrificing everything for the job.

"We got some of your files from Oklahoma finally," he said. "We're hoping you'll look through them and see if anyone rings a bell."

"Of course."

"Great. I'll take baby duty while you work on it. These files are our best lead at this point."

"I understand. I'll see what I can find out, if anything."

He moved the computer toward her. She blinked, mentally preparing herself for the task at hand. She could do this. It would be painstaking and slow, but it was nothing she couldn't handle.

But three hours later, Macy hadn't discovered anything and her neck and shoulders ached. She pushed the computer away and closed her eyes.

"No progress?" Tanner said, coming back into the room with Addie in his arms.

The baby had woken a couple hours ago, and

Tanner had entertained her with rattles and stuffed animals. He'd sat on a blanket with her and made her fly like an airplane. She'd giggled and drooled and looked at Tanner with absolute adoration in her eyes. It had been a heartwarming sight.

Macy shook her head at Tanner's question. "No. I wanted to find something. I wanted some answers. But Tanner, I couldn't find anyone who fit this mother's description. Besides it's been four months since I left. Who knows who might have gotten pregnant since I met with them—"

Tanner shifted Addie to his other hip and rested a hand on Macy's shoulder. "It's okay. I understand."

Macy hung her head, exhaustion and stress hitting her. "I don't know why she had my name in her diaper bag. I need to know my connection."

"We'll figure it out eventually."

"What if it's too late?"

"Don't think like that. We have our best guys on this case. They're working with local authorities, as well. We just have to be patient."

"Unfortunately, patience isn't one of my virtues right now. Not when my life has been turned upside down."

His gaze connected with hers. "You always did like for things to be orderly.

"Doesn't everyone?" Order helped to keep her thoughts clear and her life organized.

Tanner shrugged. "I suppose."

She rubbed her lips together, fighting her inner turmoil. "I want my life to return to normal, Tanner."

He stared at her a moment, an unreadable expression in his eyes. "I'm sorry you were pulled into this, Macy. I really am. No one anticipated this."

Macy ran a hand over her face and shook her head, realizing how whiny she sounded. She wished she could have a do-over of this conversation. She was usually much more careful about showing her emotions.

"No, I'm sorry," she said. "I'll do whatever is needed. My frustration just got the best of me."

"It's understandable."

She stood, stretching her back. "I'll search through the files again in a few minutes. Right now, I just need to clear my head."

Macy was doing what she did best under stress: cooking and baking. She'd found a few things in the refrigerator that had been stocked there. Now she had some spaghetti with a meat sauce on the stove and a chocolate cake in the oven.

Addie had gone down for a nap, and Macy

couldn't bear to simply sit around and do nothing but think.

"Something smells good," Tanner said, stepping into the room. He was freshly showered and wearing one of his typical flannel shirts—this one an especially nice shade of blue that brought out his eyes—with his jeans and cowboy boots.

Macy had also showered, trying to get rid of the smell of smoke that had saturated her hair and skin. Her hair wasn't quite dry yet and, if she didn't fix it, would end up wavy and messy. Though at the moment, she didn't care.

Tanner had been locked up in his bedroom on a phone call or something. She hadn't asked too many questions. Meanwhile, Manning and Armstrong were sleeping since they were taking the night shift this evening.

"You still like to cook when you're stressed," Tanner continued, joining her by the stove.

"Guilty as charged," she said.

"You always could make some killer meals."

She shrugged and stirred the meat sauce again. "We have to eat. I figured it might as well be something other than takeout."

"I won't argue. Can I do anything to help?"

At his suggestion, Macy's stomach clenched. She had too many memories of her and Tanner in the kitchen, cooking together, flirting, bonding. She almost couldn't stand the thought.

She cleared her throat, trying to push away the

memories before they found a warm place in her heart. "No, I think I'm good."

"Let me know if you change your mind." He flipped the TV on and moved to the breakfast bar.

Macy turned her ear toward the news report. Tanner had told her about Saul's plan to draw the bad guys out by releasing Addie's picture and find some answers in the process. She had her doubts that it would work, but at least they were trying something.

A replay of the earlier press conference showed across the screen.

Macy brought the pot over to the sink on the breakfast bar island. She drained the pasta, trying to read Tanner's expression as she did so. She couldn't, though. All she knew was that he was worried.

"Any updates?" she asked, pulling out two plates.

"Apparently, the FBI has had a whole slew of phone calls, but nothing has panned out."

"Do you think it will?"

"It's anyone's guess at this point."

She slid a plate across the counter to him at the breakfast bar, along with a glass of tea. "I'm assuming you still like sweet tea. I could be wrong, though."

"I've always been a sucker for sweet tea."

She smiled as she moved to sit across from

him. The savory scent of ground beef and garlic wafted up to her, making her stomach grumble. She couldn't wait to dig in. There'd always been something incredibly comforting about home-cooked foods.

"This looks great," he said. "You mind if we pray before we eat?"

Her cheeks flushed. Pray? Had Tanner turned over a new leaf also? That was certainly her impression. "Please do."

She closed her eyes and listened as he lifted up thanks for the provision of food and prayed for the safety of everyone involved in this investigation.

After he said amen, she picked up her fork. "I didn't realize you were a believer."

"I am. I used to think I was too smart to go to church." He glanced at her. "You know that."

She nodded. They'd had conversations about this when they'd dated. About how religion was a crutch for the weak. How it was old-fashioned, and how neither could see proof of the existence of God in their lives.

But apparently they'd both changed since then.

"What happened?" she asked, twirling some spaghetti around her fork and feeling unusually nervous.

"Working as a police officer I saw a lot of ugliness on the job. A lot of evil. And I had to believe there was more at stake here than just living and dying. A friend on the force invited me to church with him and asked me to be open-minded about it. I was, and I haven't been the same since then."

"I see." She wondered if their breakup had anything to do with it also, but she dared not ask.

He took a sip of his tea. "How about you?"

She played with her food as she tried to form her words.

"I think I came to the end of myself. Nothing was really working out the way I planned it." She swallowed hard, knowing good and well that Tanner would see through her vague answer. He'd been a big part of the change, though she didn't want to admit it.

"Go on."

She wiped her mouth, suddenly more than a little uncomfortable. "I had to come to peace with my past before I could embrace the future. It sounds a bit melodramatic, but that's really what happened. I found a church after I moved to Oklahoma and got plugged in. I made some great friends who really changed my perspective from self-reliance to God-reliance. The rest, as they say, is history."

Tanner's warm eyes met hers. "Sometimes God uses the hard times in life to draw us closer to Him."

"Even this," she said. She raised her glass of tea. Sweet tea wasn't usually an indulgence she allowed herself, but in this situation she would make an exception.

Tanner smiled gently. "Yeah, even this."

Silence passed between them as they ate. It was the first time Macy had felt a true moment of closeness with Tanner since this whole crazy ordeal had begun. And it was nice. Despite their history and everything that had happened—all the heartbreak and grief and broken dreams—maybe they could move forward as friends. Maybe what was lost could be restored.

Just as they finished eating, Addie awoke. Macy welcomed the opportunity to escape.

Because she had no right feeling this cozy with Tanner. It would only lead her to more heartache in the end. She'd be wise to remember that.

TEN

Something had cracked inside Tanner during his conversation with Macy. He couldn't explain it. He just knew that both he and Macy had changed—for the better—since they'd last spoken five years ago. Back then, they'd both been young and idealistic. They'd thought they could conquer the world. Life had taught them quite a few lessons since then. Lessons that weren't fun to learn but were necessary to growing up and maturing.

He ate his last bite of spaghetti and took his late to the sink. Somehow, he knew his relationship with Macy had just taken a positive step toward being restored. He was thankful for that. He didn't dare hope it could ever be repaired to where it had been. There was too much water under the bridge. But maybe they could at least heal from the wounds they'd each caused.

Macy emerged from the bedroom with a happy and alert Addie. His heart warmed at the sight. Macy was such a natural—so patient and unwavering in her affections.

"Look who's awake," she murmured, holding Addie's hand on one of her fingers. Her voice took on a soft, husky tone of affection.

She'd already bonded with the baby. It was both comforting and disturbing. It was good that she cared so much about the child, but it could devastate her when Addie was taken away.

Tanner wasn't sure what the outcome of all of this would be—only that he'd keep Addie alive throughout. But it could end with Addie back with her mom. With Addie in the charge of another relative or in foster care. He knew how sensitive Macy was, how tender her heart could be in situations like these—especially when it came to kids.

"You're a natural," he murmured.

As soon as he said the words, he knew they were a mistake. Macy instantly tightened and jerked her shoulder up, creating a barrier between them.

"I don't know about that," she muttered.

"I've always known you'd be a great mom, Macy." He wasn't sure why he said it. It was risky and most likely to backfire. But he wanted to explain himself. There were so many unspoken conversations between them.

"Don't feel obligated to say stuff like that,

Tanner." She turned away from him and began to warm up a bottle and prepare some rice cereal.

"I'm not obligated to say anything. I said it because I meant it."

Tanner couldn't see her reaction. Her back was toward him.

Addie stared at him over Macy's shoulder, her little eyes so wide and full of innocence.

The child really was precious. It was such a shame that she was in the middle of all this.

"Do you want me to hold her for you?" he asked.

"Sure, that would be great."

He took the infant from Macy's arms. At once, visions of the life he and Macy should have had together filled his thoughts. He hadn't let his mind go there in a long time.

Regret panged inside him. With grief over what should have been. With bitterness at the way Macy had ended things.

Addie cooed in his arms.

"You're getting hungry, aren't you?" he murmured.

She grabbed Tanner's cheek in response and stared up at him with those big eyes that melted his resolve.

"I take that as a yes," he murmured, rocking his upper body back and forth to keep her calm.

"You seem like a natural yourself," Macy said. Her voice sounded hoarse with emotion.

"Believe me, I'm not. But I'll enjoy this moment while it lasts."

That got a small smile out of Macy. She turned around with the bottle in hand and reached for Addie. "I'll take her now."

"I'll clean up from dinner then."

It seemed so natural, the two of them falling into this routine. But Tanner couldn't think like that. It was unhealthy.

Before he could start the first dish, his phone rang. It was Saul. Whenever his boss called, there was sure to be an update.

"We have a couple who came forward. They could be legit. They're coming in tomorrow morning. I'd like for you and Macy to be here."

"But sir, I don't know that it's safe—"

"We're going to send another agent to help with Addie. She'll stay at the safe house. We'll take precautions. Understand?"

"Yes, sir."

"Great. I'll see you then."

Macy's nerves were shot the next morning as she walked with Tanner into the FBI's Houston field office. She was nervous about leaving Addie, even though Cara Meekins, the agent they'd sent to stay there, seemed perfectly respectable. Macy had bonded with the child and felt protective of her.

Then there was Tanner.

Macy couldn't deny that they'd shared a moment yesterday. Finding out he'd become a believer also changed a lot of things. She was reminded of God's command to forgive.

All the hurts she'd stored away for so long had continued to build resentment in her. She knew she had to let go. But it was so scary. It meant stepping into the unknown. It meant opening oneself up to hurt again.

Then there was this whole meeting. Who were these people who claimed they knew Addie? Macy's gut told her that things could turn ugly. She would be slow to trust anyone in this circumstance.

She glanced around quickly. They were in Tanner's office. She noted the well-used Bible on his desk. The mountain picture with a Scripture verse at the bottom.

He wasn't lying when he said he'd become a Christian, and he wasn't afraid to let anyone know it. There was a lot to be said for that.

There were also awards hanging up, and a picture of Tanner with his granddad. Everything was neat and orderly, just as Macy would expect it to be.

"You ready for this?" Tanner placed his hand on her back.

She nearly jumped out of her skin. She must have flinched so harshly that he misread her and quickly pulled his hand away. "Yeah, yeah. I'm ready. I think."

"You've got good observation skills. I want to hear your thoughts."

She nodded, feeling like she'd been caught up in a whirlwind. "Of course."

"I'm going to get you situated outside in the observation area. It's better if they don't see your face, just in case."

"I understand." And she was partly relieved that she didn't have to participate in the conflict that could take place. She preferred having time just to observe and form opinions.

She took her place behind the tinted glass. She could see in, but those in the room couldn't see out.

Another agent brought her a cup of coffee, and Macy attempted to drink it. But her hands were shaking too badly. Even the normally comforting smell of coffee only served to turn her stomach right now.

What would today's outcome be?

Macy stared at the meeting room. A dark mahogany table with six leather chairs surrounding it sat in the middle. Dark burgundy walls made the room feel cozier than it actually was. A watercooler was in one corner, and there were no windows. She was sure each aspect of the room had been carefully chosen.

Tanner and Saul stood against one wall, chatting with each other. Saul looked as uptight as ever—as he should be in this situation, Macy supposed. The man reminded her of one of her psychology professors with his salt-and-pepper beard and bald head.

A moment later, a man and woman entered the room. Tanner and Saul shook their hands and directed them to seats across from them.

Macy observed the couple. They were probably in their early thirties and well dressed. The woman had red hair that was smoothed back in neat curls, wore a fitted suit with pearls and heels, and gave off a professional vibe. The man wore khakis with a shirt and tie. He had dark hair and the shadow of a beard.

Both appeared apprehensive, which would be normal under these circumstances—if they were telling the truth or not. However, if they were lying, they'd probably try to conceal their deceit by subduing their nerves more.

Macy put a mental check in the "honest" category. She had to be objective here and not let her emotions lead her. It never ended well when she let that happen.

"Thanks for coming," Saul started.

They were all seated around the table. Both Saul and Tanner rested their hands. Body language 101 on how to look non-intimidating? Maybe. She knew the FBI did quite a bit of training on these things.

Macy looked down at the dossier she'd been given. Their names were Deborah Graham and Mike Devry. They were from Dallas. He worked in finance, and she was an interior designer. Though they weren't married, they'd been in a relationship for seven years and lived together.

"What makes you think this baby might be related to you?" Saul continued.

The two exchanged a glance with each other.

"We believe she's my niece." Deborah hooked a stray hair behind her ear.

"And why is that?" Tanner asked.

"Her mom, Michelle Nixon, had a baby six months ago," Mike said. "She was unstable and didn't let us see her very often. We haven't heard from Michelle in a week. We've gone by her place, and it's locked up. Frankly, we're very worried. When I saw the news story, it was my first ray of hope."

"How is Michelle related to you?" Saul shifted in his chair.

"She's my sister," Deborah said.

Why wasn't Deborah more concerned about her sister? The question bugged Macy. All the woman's concern seemed to be focused on the child.

"What can you tell us about this baby?" Saul said.

"Her name is Bella, but Michelle liked to call her Addie," Deborah said. "Michelle's ex insisted on the name Bella, but my sister never really liked that name. Anyway, Addie is six months old, and she's got the most adorable dark curls. Last time we saw her she had two teeth. I suppose she could have more by now, though."

That was all good, but they could have gathered some of that information from the picture the FBI had released to the media. The number of teeth could be guessed based on basic knowledge about infants.

"Where was she born?" Tanner asked.

"Outside of Houston," Deborah said. "We can give you the name of the hospital, if you'd like, as well as the date of her birth."

"That would be great," Saul said. "You have no idea where your sister is?"

"No, we have no idea," Deborah said with a frown. "Like we said, she's a bit unstable, and we haven't heard from her in a week. It's not unusual for her to take off without telling anyone. But she's not even answering her cell phone, nor has she paid her bills this month."

A wrinkle formed between Tanner's eyes. "How do you know that?"

"Well, Michelle's mailbox was full," Deborah said. "Overflowing. I know we shouldn't have looked, but we were worried. I looked through her mail to see if it offered any clues. I saw a lot of bills."

"You never thought of calling the police?" Tanner asked.

"Like we said, this is typical," Mike chimed in. "But when we saw that picture we got worried. We began to wonder if something had happened. Michelle would never leave her baby unless she was desperate. We're anxious to have Addie back in the family."

"We'll have to verify your story first, of course," Saul said.

"Of course." Mike nodded. He paused. "Is she…okay?"

"We assure you that she's safe, and she's being taken care of until all of this is resolved. Her safety is of utmost importance to us."

Tanner stood. "Saul is going to get your information. Thank you both for coming in."

"Thank you." Deborah ran a tissue under her eyes, as if the emotional stress of the moment was more than she could take.

Tanner stepped into the room where Macy waited and took her arm, leading her down the hallway at a quick pace.

"What are you doing?" she asked.

"We're going to follow them when they leave the field office. We need to get out to our car and be ready."

Tanner replayed the conversation with Deborah and Mike as they climbed into the car. He was interested to hear Macy's take on all of it. But right now, he needed to be in place to tail them. He had to see if the couple was telling the truth, and this was one part of doing so.

He started the car and moved toward the gate. Another agent had already informed him which vehicle belonged to the couple. As soon as the two ventured out of the parking lot, Tanner would ease behind them and see where they were going.

"Cara—Agent Meekins—texted me, by the way," Tanner told Macy. "Addie is doing fine."

"That's good to know. I've been worried about her. Which is ridiculous." She rubbed her hands together nervously in her lap.

"No, it's not. You two have bonded."

"Yes, we have. In one way, I feel responsible for her, like she's my own flesh and blood."

He glanced at Macy. She'd transformed today from the youthful, laidback Macy at the safe house to the professional Dr. Mills. She'd worn some neat jeans with a button-up shirt. Her hair was pulled back into a knot and she wore her glasses. That familiar scent of fresh cotton filled the car. Honestly, both sides of her were very attractive.

"Well, what did you think of Deborah and Mike?" Tanner asked, trying to keep his thoughts focused.

Macy pressed her lips together, her gaze narrowing with focus and reflection. "I thought their answers were vague. Some things they said could have simply been good guesses."

"I agree. Nothing they said offered definitive proof that this baby is their niece."

"No, there wasn't. I guess the proof will be finding out if their story checks out."

"We have agents looking into that." He sat up straight and pointed to a red car in the distance. "There they are now."

Macy gripped the armrest, as if bracing herself for whatever was about to come. "You really think following them will offer answers?"

"It's better to find out now than later. Later, we may not be able to track them down at all."

"Let's do this, then."

Tanner eased out behind the car, keeping a safe distance between his vehicle and the red sedan. The windows in the FBI vehicle were tinted and the vehicle itself unassuming. If he played this right, Deborah and Mike should never know they were being followed.

They traveled toward the downtown area. This could make things more complicated, Tanner mused. Traffic could be a friend or an enemy.

The number of cars on the road thickened the closer they got to the city. Tanner remained at least three cars behind the couple so he wouldn't tip them off.

"Do you think they know they're being followed?" Macy asked, still looking slightly uncomfortable. None of this was exactly in her wheelhouse.

"They shouldn't. Although, if they're guilty of lying to us, they'll likely be more suspicious and watch their backs." He followed the sedan and turned onto a side street. His muscles tensed. Between the heavy traffic and the red lights, this was going to be a challenge.

Macy craned her neck to see over the cars in front of them. "I can't see them anymore."

Tanner scanned the road. "There they are!"

He made a quick turn into a side street as he caught a glimpse of the red sedan. He could barely see them ahead, but if he lost them now, he wasn't sure he'd be able to find them again.

Traffic was bumper to bumper. He wove in and out of cars. But just as he reached an intersection, the light turned red. The car in front of him braked.

Tanner stopped only inches from the other car's bumper. His gaze darted from left to right. There was no way he could pull out without endangering other people.

He bit back his frustration.

He'd lost Deborah and Mike.

Or had Deborah and Mike lost them?

ELEVEN

"They're gone," Tanner muttered.

"It could be a coincidence," Macy offered. "Traffic was heavy."

"Could be," Tanner said, his jaw tightening. This wasn't the ending he'd envisioned. Yet he couldn't justify a high-speed chase in order to keep up with Mike and Deborah. There wasn't enough proof they were being deceitful, and too many innocent people would have been at risk. "We should head back."

"I'm ready to see Addie again," Macy said.

"I don't need to warn you about the dangers of getting too close, do I?" Tanner asked as he headed back to the safe house.

Her cheeks flushed. "No, of course not."

"I didn't think so. But I wanted to check, just in case."

Thirty minutes later, he pulled up to the gate and threw his sedan into Park. He punched in the security code, but nothing happened.

He clenched his jaw as tension gripped him.

The only reason for this gate not to open was if the code had been changed or if the power had been cut. He didn't like either of those options.

"It's not working?" Macy asked through the open door.

"No, it's not." He pulled out his phone and tried to call Cara. She didn't answer. Neither did Manning or Armstrong.

Tanner's muscles went from tense to downright knotted. Something was wrong. Majorly wrong.

He pulled out an extra gun from his ankle holster and slapped it into Macy's hand. "Use this if you have to. Keep the doors locked. Understand?"

Macy's eyes widened, but she nodded. "Got it."

"You remember how to shoot?"

Her cheeks warmed. Was she remembering the lessons he'd given her in college? Anytime he mentioned their past, she got that deer-in-the-headlights expression.

"Yeah, I remember."

He patted the top of the car. "Stay safe."

Alarm pulsed through his blood as he approached the fence. Despite the measures they'd taken to ensure the security of the house on the other side, every instinct inside him screamed that Addie was in danger.

Agent Meekins was capable of handling herself. But when she didn't answer her phone, concern had ricocheted through Tanner.

Maybe Cara's phone was dead. Maybe she'd left it out of reach.

Tanner didn't believe either of those things, though. All agents were instructed to keep their phones charged, near them and to always answer.

His boots scraped across the gravel driveway, and he felt the gun in his holster as he stretched to full height. With the sun beating down on his shoulders, he climbed the fence and landed hard on the other side.

He studied the area, looking for a sign of danger, but saw nothing except the evergreen trees surrounding the gravel driveway, which curved before the house could be seen. The scene looked ironically peaceful and in direct contradiction to what his gut told him.

He hurried up the lane and around the bend of trees. The house came into view, but Tanner paused at the sight of it.

The front door was cracked open.

His pulse rate quickened.

His team would never leave the front door open. If there was one thing the agents weren't, it was careless.

Tanner drew his gun and called for backup before pressing forward. Dread pooled in his stomach when he thought about what might have happened here.

Please Lord, let me be overreacting.

He knew he wasn't. He glanced around, looking for a sign of trouble. Two FBI sedans were still parked out back, and no other vehicles were in sight. He surveyed the trees surrounding the property but saw no one and nothing suspicious.

Carefully, Tanner stepped onto the rustic, wooden porch, certain his footsteps didn't make a sound. He paused as the skin on the back of his neck crawled. Slowly, he turned, glancing at the woods again.

He saw no one, yet he felt certain that someone was watching him.

His instincts went on full alert.

Using all his skills and training, he nudged the front door open. Silence greeted him.

The stillness was not a good sign. If Cara was safe and everything was normal, there would be laughter and chatter and maybe even some nursery rhymes.

Tanner stepped inside, soaking in the empty house. A baby rattle lay on the floor. One of the blankets was strewn across the brown leather couch as if someone had been taking a nap. Fresh coffee—he could smell it—waited in the percolator on the kitchen counter.

What was going on?

Remaining on the edge of the room, Tanner

continued deeper into the house. As he crossed into the kitchen and looked beyond the breakfast bar, he froze.

Cara.

She laid sprawled on the floor by the back door. Blood pooled near her head, and her gun lay on the tile floor beside her hand.

He rushed toward her and put his finger to the pulse at her neck. It was still there but barely. He radioed headquarters, requesting an ambulance.

"Come on, Cara," he muttered. "Hold on."

There was nothing he could do to help her, he realized.

While he waited for the medics to arrive, he had to figure out what happened here and check to see if the killer remained in the house. One other thing took top priority, however.

Baby Addie.

Where was she? And where were Manning and Armstrong?

He paused as he heard a subtle rustling sound. Was someone still in the house? Just waiting to strike?

He raised his gun, ready to use it if he had to.

Carefully, he maneuvered himself toward the hallway. Each step was purposeful and careful. He couldn't afford to mess this up. Too many people were depending on him.

Tanner reached the downstairs bedroom. He lingered by the doorway before propelling himself inside. He scanned the room, but nothing out of the ordinary struck him. Carefully, he walked across the room and pulled up the bed-cover, checking beneath it.

Empty.

His heart pounding against his rib cage, he opened the closet door. A baby stared back at him from the corner. His adrenaline surged when he realized it was a doll.

The space was empty.

Tanner followed the same procedure, room after room. No one was here. Not even Manning or Armstrong.

So what had that sound been? And what about the feeling he had outside? The feeling of being watched?

He hoped backup arrived soon. He prayed Macy stayed in the sedan like he'd told her.

Another noise swished inside the house. His eyes zeroed in on the hallway wall. No, it wasn't the wall. It was a doorway made to look like part of the wall, he realized. Why hadn't he seen that earlier?

Cautiously, Tanner walked toward it. Not see-ing a handle, he nudged it, and the door popped open as if spring-loaded.

A dark closet greeted him, full of coats, and a vacuum cleaner. He moved some of the gar-ments aside, looking for the source of that noise.

His breath caught when he saw something

on the floor. Addie. The baby was tucked away safe in her car seat. Wide awake and seemingly happy, she tugged at the coats as if they were part of a mobile placed above a crib. What he'd heard was the sound of the hangers hitting each other.

He tucked his gun away and bent down, carefully lifting the child from her car seat and holding her close in his arms.

The air left his lungs as relief filled him. The baby was safe. But they weren't out of the woods yet, so to speak. The bad guys were most likely planning their next attack, and Tanner would have to constantly be on guard.

The good news was that Cara had insured that Addie wasn't taken. She'd put her own life on the line to do so.

But for how long would that be true? How were they going to protect this baby that someone else was so desperate to get their hands on?

Macy gripped the gun and lifted a prayer. She didn't want to have to use this weapon. But she wouldn't hesitate to protect herself. To protect baby Addie.

Anxiety coiled in her as a bad feeling continued to churn in her gut. Something was seriously amiss here, and she didn't know what to do about it. She liked to fix things. To make people's problems better.

But here she was locked in the sedan, crouched low in her seat, and feeling helpless.

There was one thing she could do. One very important thing. She could pray.

Dear Lord, protect Addie. Protect Tanner. Protect the other agents. Please.

Movement in the distance caught her eye, and her grip on the gun tightened. It was two men walking down the road.

She peered up again, trying to get a better look.

Wait...was that Manning and Armstrong?

What was going on?

Once their faces came into focus, she opened the car door and rushed across the gravel at the side of the road to meet them. She was desperate to know if they were okay, to learn what happened.

She soaked in how they both looked dazed and out of sorts. "What's going on? Are you okay?"

"We were ambushed," Manning said, rubbing his temple. "Put in the back of a van then shoved out on the side of the road."

"That's terrible. I'm glad you're both alive." Her concern spiraled to a new level. "Where's Addie?"

"We don't know," Armstrong said. "Cara was inside with her when we stepped out to investigate a noise outside. It was all a ploy to get us away from the house."

Worry gripped her again. How had their location been discovered...again?

"Macy, over here," a familiar voice called.

She swung her head toward the sound and saw Tanner standing at the gate...with Addie cradled in his arms.

Relief flushed through her. She put the gun on the car hood and rushed toward them. She took Addie into her arms and held the baby close, relishing the clean fresh scent of her skin and hair. In response, Addie cooed and grabbed for Macy's locks.

"How's Cara?" Macy asked, still not letting down her guard.

"She was shot, but she's alive. But an ambulance is on its way." Tanner turned toward Manning and Armstrong. "Are you guys okay?"

They nodded. "Yes, sir."

"Where have you been?"

"We were ambushed, sir. But we managed to get away."

"I'm glad to hear that, and we'll debrief later. For now, I need you two to stay here with Cara. It's not safe for Addie to be here. We don't know where the bad guys are. We need to get out of here before someone tries to make us victims again. It's too big a risk."

Manning nodded. "Of course."

"You two will be okay?" Tanner continued.

"Yes, sir," Armstrong said.

Tanner put his hand on Macy's back. "Okay, we've got to go then."

Macy saw that Tanner had grabbed the car seat and diaper bag. They quickly loaded everything into the vehicle and then started down the road.

"I'm sorry about Cara," she said through the tension-stretched quiet.

She could tell he was deep in thought, and that he was disturbed about where all of this was leading. He took his job to protect others—even his colleagues—very seriously.

Tanner bit down. "Me, too. I think she'll be okay, though. But, right now, I have a mission. I've got to keep this baby safe."

"I understand." Macy shook her head as her thoughts pressed down on her, feeling like she was going under an emotional wave that kept hitting her again and again. "How do these people keep figuring out where we are?"

"That's what I'd like to know." His jaw flexed like it always did when he wasn't happy. "I don't even have any good guesses at this point."

Silence stretched between them again as the miles rolled past. Addie played with a little toy that was attached to the car seat and seemed content for the moment. But Macy had too many unknowns, too many questions. Contentment felt far away from her.

She cleared her throat. "Where are we going?"

"I don't know yet," Tanner said.

She studied the set of his jaw, the way he focused on the road straight ahead, his tight grip on the steering wheel. "There's something you're not saying, Tanner."

He snapped out of his ultra-focused mode and rubbed the back of his neck. He still didn't say anything for a moment. Finally, he drew in a deep breath. "I wonder if there's a leak within the FBI."

Macy gasped at his words. "Really?"

"Yeah, really. I don't know how else these guys could keep finding us. They have to have an inside connection."

"Who do you think it is?"

"There's only a handful of people who know where we're staying. Manning, Armstrong, Saul, Cara, and maybe an administrator."

Each of their faces flashed through Macy's mind until she shivered. "I hate to think that any of them would betray the FBI."

"Me, too."

Her throat suddenly felt dry and tight. She glanced out the window, the landscape around them looking more ominous by the moment. It was like she couldn't trust anyone or anything... except maybe Tanner.

"What are we going to do, Tanner?" she asked.

He glanced at her. "We may have to go rogue."

TWELVE

As Tanner cruised down the road, his phone rang. He glanced at the screen and saw that it was Saul. Even though he'd just declared the need to go rogue, Tanner knew he had to play it cool right now in order to not raise suspicions.

"Hey, Saul," Tanner answered through the Bluetooth in his car. "What's going on?"

"Cara's going to be okay." Saul's voice came through. "She has a surface wound and will spend some time under observation, but doctors aren't expecting any complications."

Relief filled him. "That's great news."

"I knew you'd want to know."

Tanner kept his eyes on the road, his adrenaline still pumping. "Any idea how these guys found us?"

"That's what we're still trying to figure out."

He'd been hoping for a more definite answer. "No clues?"

"Not at this point," Saul said. "We're investigating to see if there was a tracker planted somehow. It's the only thing that makes sense to us at this point."

Now that was an interesting idea. Interesting and highly disturbing. "Are you checking the place for anything that may have slipped past us?"

"As we speak. I also wanted to let you know that we just got a report on Deborah Graham and Mike Devry, the supposed relatives of baby Addie."

"And?" Tanner braced himself for what he might hear.

"They appear to be legit," Saul said. "Deborah's sister is named Michelle Nixon. She really did have a baby about six months ago, and no one has seen either of them in a couple of weeks. We're still tracking down details, though. Nothing is confirmed, though initial analysis seems to be positive."

"Where are they from?"

"Down near Galveston," Saul said.

"Even if their story is true, that still doesn't explain the extreme measures someone is going through to get this child," Tanner said.

"Maybe the mom got herself into trouble. Maybe she owes some drug lords and they want the baby as payment."

"These guys seem a little smarter than your average drug lords."

"I agree. But that's the only logical conclusion we're able to draw right now. We'll let you know as more information comes in. We're in the process of getting another safe house set up for you."

Tanner wanted to tell him to not bother. But he didn't. He had to be more subtle than that. "I'll lay low until then."

"Sounds good."

He ended the call and placed his phone on the seat beside him. His mind reviewed what Saul had told him as he continued down the road.

Macy shivered beside him. "I don't like the sound of any of this."

"Neither do I."

"Are you really waiting for them to assign another safe house?"

He shook his head. "Of course not. But I've got to figure out what we're going to do in the meantime."

"You always have a plan," she said.

"I usually do."

"I don't like the sound of that, either."

Tanner glanced in the rearview mirror and saw no one. So he wasn't being followed. But what if someone was tracking him through another means? He didn't want to think that was possible, but it was.

They needed to ditch their possessions and get a clean start—a totally clean start.

When he came to the first shopping center, he

stopped. Part one of his plan started here. But they had to act quick.

"What are we doing?" Macy asked.

"We've got to buy everything new. Clothes. Baby supplies. New phones even. We're going to lose these people once and for all."

Two hours later, they had gotten rid of all their old stuff. Macy had an entirely new outfit. Addie had a new car seat, new pacifier and new bottles. The only thing that stayed the same was Tanner's boots and cowboy hat, but he had thoroughly investigated both of them. He'd also carefully checked the car to make sure there was no tracking device there.

Macy wasn't sure how she felt as she climbed back in the car. All of this seemed like something from a movie, like it couldn't possibly be her real life.

Before they left, Tanner grabbed some food at a fast-food joint. The entire time they were in the drive-through line, he continually scanned the area. Macy could tell he was on edge.

Finally, they hit the road again, though Macy had no idea where they were going.

She leaned back in her seat and took a bite of her chicken sandwich. She hadn't realized how hungry she was. She sat in the back seat with Addie, though part of her wished she could sit up front with Tanner. She wanted to talk with him.

To really talk. To see his eyes when she asked questions. But that wasn't an option right now.

When she finished, she put a hand on Addie's belly, trying to keep her settled. The baby's agitation certainly didn't help the stress of the situation. But all Macy could do was try to keep the child soothed. This was hard on all of them.

"So, what now?" Macy asked, feeling the first signs of real exhaustion pressing on her. She'd hoped Tanner might share this information on his own but apparently not.

"We're going to my friend's house."

Surprise rippled through her. "Really?"

He nodded. "Yeah, really. He's one of the few people I can trust in this situation. We're almost at his place now."

Fifteen minutes later, they pulled up to a ranch-style structure located in the Texas countryside.

"Wait here," Tanner said.

He hopped out and darted up to the door.

Macy's eyes widened when she saw the man who answered.

Devin Blankenship. Tanner's best friend.

Macy hadn't seen him in years. Back in grad school, she'd spent endless hours hanging out with him and Tanner. He'd almost felt like a brother.

Devin was the former high school football player who'd forgone a contract in order to join the police. He was still built like a linebacker. His dark hair was a little thinner now.

The man had always been a straight shooter, and Macy had always appreciated his honesty.

Except right now, she wasn't sure if she was ready to face it. She was certain he'd have harsh words for her after she'd broken up with his best friend.

Memories of the past rushed back to her, hitting her like a tidal wave. They'd all had some really good times together. They'd not only had cookouts and game nights, but they'd gone hiking together and spent a week at the beach playing volleyball and body surfing.

This wasn't going to get any easier, was it? She looked down at Addie. The baby gripped her finger and tried to shove it in her mouth.

"We're going to get through this," Macy whispered, pulling her finger away from Addie's lips. "I promise."

Tanner jogged back to the car and opened Macy's door. "Come on in."

Still feeling shell-shocked, she stepped outside. Tanner grabbed Addie's car seat, not even flinching at the weight.

"We'll come back and get the rest of our stuff later," he said. "Let's get out of this cold for now."

Anxiety tightened Macy's gut as she walked with Tanner toward the front door. How would

Devin react to seeing her? With the same resentment she'd expected to feel from Tanner?

As Devin opened the door, she pulled her gaze up to meet his and swallowed hard.

"Devin," she said with a polite nod.

"If it isn't Macy Mills," he said. "It's been a long time."

"It really has."

To her surprise, he pulled her into a hug. "It's great to see you. Come on in."

While Tanner and Devin talked in the kitchen, Macy gave Addie a bath and fed her a bottle. When she got the baby down for a nap, Macy took a shower and cleaned herself up. Finally, she felt halfway alive and ready to face whatever was next.

The scent of savory beef greeted her when she stepped out of the spare bedroom. She followed the aroma into the kitchen, where Tanner and Devin sat at the table drinking coffee.

Tanner stood when he saw her, his eyes widening. "Feeling better?"

She nodded and pushed a strand of hair behind her ear. "Yes, I am. And Addie is asleep."

"I'm going to take a note from your book and go get cleaned up. You two will be okay?" Tanner asked, looking back and forth between the two of them.

Macy glanced at Devin, feeling a touch of

nerves at the possibility of a confrontation, at worst, or an unpleasant conversation, at best.

"Of course," she finally said, rubbing her hands on her jeans.

But deep inside Macy had prepared herself for a verbal lashing. The man was loyal. He always had been, and Macy didn't expect anything to change.

Tanner took a step toward the hallway and paused in front of her. "We'll eat dinner and then we're going to head out."

"That sounds good," Macy said.

As soon as he left, a moment of awkward silence filled the room.

"Can I get you some coffee?" Devin stood and walked toward the counter.

"That sounds great. Thank you." She pulled out a seat at the table and waited awkwardly.

He got up to pour her a cup and then set it in front of her. She wrapped her fingers around the warm ceramic mug, wishing she could transport herself from this moment.

Devin stared at her from across the table. "So how are you doing, Macy?"

She nodded slowly as she considered her words. "Just fine, I suppose. If you don't count this current situation, that is."

"Of course. Why'd you come back to this area? I thought you were gone for good."

"To be closer to my family. Oklahoma was always supposed to be short-term." She cleared her throat and took a quick sip of her coffee. "How about you? Still a cop?"

"Yes, ma'am." He tipped an invisible hat toward her before leaning closer. "Look, I know we're dancing around the elephant in the room right now. I always find it better to get these things out in the open. You and Tanner are working together again, huh?"

"Not really by either of our choice. Circumstances kind of threw us together."

He leveled his gaze with hers. "He still hasn't gotten over your breakup, you know."

Macy scoffed, knowing an exaggeration when she heard one. "Of course he has. He's always been all about his job. I'm sure it's made him a lot happier than I ever did." As she said the words, her father's image filled her mind. All men were alike, right?

She knew they weren't. But maybe deep down inside she'd believed that lie.

"Is that really what you think? I thought you knew him better than that."

Her cheeks flushed. "I know him well enough to know he lives for law enforcement."

Devin sat back and rubbed his jaw. "You should really talk to him."

"I'm not sure what good it would accomplish. The past is the past." She heard the fallacy in her words. She counseled her clients about the importance of dealing with their pasts all the time. Why was it so hard to take her own advice?

"Maybe it would just offer some closure." He shifted. "I always thought the two of you were good together."

"We've both changed a lot since those days, Devin." She stared into her coffee. "Sometimes time really doesn't heal all wounds, even if we'd like to believe it does."

THIRTEEN

Tanner noticed how quiet Macy was as they headed down the road after a dinner of pot roast and potatoes. What exactly had she and Devin talked about? He wanted to ask, but they had more important matters at hand right now.

Tanner had gone through the proper steps to ensure they wouldn't be followed. He'd switched out his FBI vehicle for one of Devin's cars. He'd left his FBI-issued cell in the car and bought a burner phone instead. If there was a tracking device in any of their possessions, they should be clear of it now. He'd left both the car and the phone in a parking lot, which would make their current location harder to trace.

All of this could be enough to make Tanner lose his job. But he had to do whatever was necessary to help protect this child. As the stakes continued to rise, he couldn't be complicit in a kidnapping—or a murder.

"Where are we going?" Macy asked, staring out her window and seeming especially melancholy.

He hated to think he had anything to do with her sadness. He'd known it would be hard for Macy to see Devin. His friend had always been a direct kind of guy.

"Devin's family has a farmhouse. They said we could stay there for a while."

She clasped her hands on her lap. "Do you think anyone will find us there?"

He readjusted his grip on the steering wheel, pushing aside the nudge of anxiety he felt. He'd been through a lot of situations during his career with law enforcement, but nothing like this.

"I hope not," he finally said. "But we've got to be prepared in case they do."

"I'm not cut out for this kind of thing, Tanner." She rubbed her arms and broke her trance-like gaze out the window.

He saw a flash of vulnerability in her eyes. It was something he'd only caught quick glimpses of since they'd reconnected. She guarded herself a little too well sometimes. The last time he'd seen that look…they'd been engaged.

Against his better instincts, he reached out and squeezed her hand. "I think you're holding up great."

She swung her head back and forth, released his hand and rubbed her temples. "We still have no idea why my name was scribbled on some paper and placed in the baby's diaper bag. That was the whole reason you came to me—to get my help. I don't feel like I'm being much assistance at all. I'm just another complication."

"You've been a huge help with Addie. I don't know what I would have done without you."

"You would have managed."

"I happen to think that everything happens for a purpose."

She glanced up at him. "Even this?"

"Even this. In Ecclesiastes 3, it says, 'Everything that happens in this world happens at the time God chooses. He sets the time for birth and the time for death…the time for killing and the time for healing.'"

"That's a good reminder," Macy said. "There is a time for everything. A right time and a wrong time."

Tanner glanced behind him, trying to make sure no one was following them. Everything appeared clear.

Now he had to concentrate solely on keeping Addie and Macy safe.

After Addie was asleep, Macy crept downstairs. She'd hardly a chance to take in the farmhouse when they arrived.

Addie had been hungry and in need of a diaper change, and then Macy had set her down on a blanket for some tummy time. She hadn't realized just how demanding a six-month-old could be. But every moment was worth it. Seeing Addie smile made all the sacrifices worth it.

Macy glanced around now. The two-story home had clapboard siding, wood floors and updated furniture. The place was surprisingly large and spacious and even had a porch swing. If circumstances were different, Macy would definitely be enjoying that. In fact, she'd had dreams of living in a place like this. Fixing it up with shiplap and shabby chic furniture. She wanted a slew of kids, a family dog or two, and maybe even a mini-farm.

From what she'd observed on the way in, it appeared to be located on a large piece of property. The terrain was mostly flat with a few trees on the perimeter. At least the wide-open spaces would afford them a chance to see anyone coming. Tanner had stowed the car away in the garage, and Macy herself had verified that no one had been behind them on the long country lane leading here.

Macy found Tanner sitting on the couch with a computer he'd picked up at a pawn shop. He offered a soft smile when he saw her and patted the space beside him. With a touch of hesitancy, she sat down.

At once, his familiar scent hit her again. She'd thought she was over her reaction to the man, but apparently she wasn't. Because if she closed her eyes, she could let herself get lost in that leathery aroma.

"What are you doing?" She glanced at the computer and brought her thoughts back into focus.

Tanner frowned before saying softly, "I'm looking into the deaths of women of childbearing age in this area within the past four days."

His words caused emotion to catch in Macy's throat. "That's…sobering."

"I know. But it's reality. Unfortunately."

The thought hovered in her mind. What if Addie's mom was dead? What would happen to Addie then? Would she go into the child welfare system?

The thought was unbearable. She couldn't let herself dwell on it now though. She had other concerns to address first.

She shifted and pulled a pillow onto her lap. The action had been initially subconscious, though she realized exactly what she was doing. Creating a barrier between her and Tanner. Protecting herself. Putting up boundaries.

She licked her lips before asking, "You really think Addie's mom is dead?"

"I think it's a possibility we have to explore."

She peered at the computer. "How'd you get those files?"

"Devin helped me. He's sent over what he's found so far, and I've been eliminating a majority of the victims. Most of these women have been identified."

"Are there any who haven't?"

"Just two right now," Tanner said.

That seemed like a step in the right direction. "Do you have their photos?"

Tanner clicked on something. "Well, there's this woman. She died of a drug overdose. From what I can tell, she shows no signs of having given birth over the past year."

"The second one?"

"The second one is more complicated. She was killed in an auto accident. Hit-and-run. She's... unrecognizable."

Macy sucked in a quick breath. "What do they know about her?"

"She's twenty-three. The car she was in was stolen, apparently."

Macy let that sink in. "She could be our best possibility yet, Tanner."

"I agree."

"How will authorities identify her?"

"Usually in cases like this someone will come forward because a loved one is missing. Otherwise, the medical examiner will try to match fingerprints and dental records."

"Do you know how soon they'll know?"

"Any day now. So until then, we wait."

"Waiting is so hard," Macy muttered.

"Yes, it is."

A moment of silence stretched between them. Macy looked at her fingers in her lap, trying to formulate her thoughts. There was no easy way to broach the subject that had been on her mind since her talk with Devin. But maybe it was time. She was a psychologist. She taught people how to come to terms with their pasts. Now she needed to listen to her own advice.

"Tanner, I'm sorry I left you nothing but a note to break up with you," she started, her voice raw and scratchy with emotion. "It was a poor choice."

His eyebrows flickered up. He closed the laptop and turned to face her. "I…uh… I wasn't expecting you to say that. But thank you."

She'd already dived in. She had to finish this now. "I knew if I tried to have a conversation with you face-to-face that I'd change my mind. So I did the cowardly thing instead. I left the note and got out of town."

"I understand that you wanted to go to grad school to get your doctorate. And everything that happened…well, it gave you that chance." His voice sounded just as tight as hers.

She shook her head, wishing he wasn't making it this easy on her. "I didn't really care about getting my doctorate in Oklahoma, Tanner."

"What do you mean?" His eyes narrowed with thought.

Anxiety suddenly got the best of her, and

all she wanted to do was get out of here. Now. She unfolded her legs from beneath her, ready to spring up. "You know what? Never mind. I shouldn't have brought this up."

Tanner gently laid a hand on her arm before she could flee "No, I want to know. Please."

She eased herself back onto the couch and licked her lips. She'd dreaded this moment for a long time and had built it up to be insurmountable. She just needed to get this over with.

"Pruett talked to me," she started, forcing her eyes to meet Tanner's.

Confusion washed over his features. "Pruett? The guy who was in police academy with me?"

She nodded. "Yeah, he told me about your conversation with him. I didn't want to stand in the way of your dreams, Tanner. That's why—"

"Wait, wait, wait." He raised a hand to halt the conversation. Tension, confusion and maybe a touch of anger tightened his face. "I don't remember a conversation with Pructt. And what do you mean stand in the way of my dreams? How in the world were you doing that? You were my dream, Macy."

Her cheeks warmed at the sincerity in his words. All her thoughts disappeared for a moment. But she couldn't get tangled up in all her emotions. She needed to get this conversation over with.

"He told me why you proposed," she finally

said, her voice cracking. She didn't want to relive that conversation. But she had to.

"And why was that?" He leaned forward, his elbows propped on his legs and intently watching her. Waiting for her response.

Her eyes met his. "Because I was pregnant."

FOURTEEN

"Your pregnancy obviously sped up how I thought everything would play out," Tanner said, still trying to comprehend what Macy was telling him. This had been the last thing he'd expected to hear. "But that wasn't the only reason I proposed."

Macy shook her head, her shoulders slumped as if the emotional burden of this conversation was too heavy to carry. "If you only married me because I was pregnant, I would always wonder if you really loved me or if you'd just married me because it was the right thing. I'd wondered about it before, but then when Pruett told me that…"

"It played right into all your fears." Tanner frowned.

She drew in a long, deep breath. "He told me you weren't going to be able to go to the FBI Academy. You would resent me for that. You may not have thought so at the time, but in the end, you would have."

"I should have been the judge of that."

Anger fought to burst to life inside him, but Tanner used every ounce of restraint to hold it back. Anger would do no good right now, and would only serve to silence Macy. He didn't want that. She'd been silent for five years.

Macy glanced down at her lap again and rubbed her lips together, another wave of melancholy seeming to wash over her. "Then I lost the baby. The truth is I was devastated."

She dragged her gaze up to meet his. "I've always wanted a family. I've always felt like I was traversing through life by myself. As you know, my mom died when I was young and then my dad buried himself in his work. My sister is considerably older than me, and she's busy with her own family."

"I know."

"Then I met you, and I didn't feel alone." Her voice cracked with emotion. "When I got pregnant, images of having the family I'd always dreamed about filled my thoughts. I didn't really care about my degree anymore even. Suddenly, life seemed really clear."

"I know losing the baby was hard on you, Macy."

She swung her head back and forth before pinching the skin between her eyes. "It was ridiculous, wasn't it? I mean, we weren't ready for a baby. It was all an accident."

Tanner grabbed her hand and squeezed it, wishing he could relieve some of her pain. "The baby would have been a blessing, despite the circumstances."

She wiped away a tear that had welled up and trickled down her flushed cheek, dragged in a ragged breath and seemed to take a moment to compose herself. "You had every right to mourn," he continued. "That was our child. I don't care what anyone else said." Tanner shifted and lowered his voice. "I wish you'd talked to me, Macy."

Macy pulled her hand away, his words seeming to snap her out of her vulnerable state. "It doesn't matter now, right? Everything worked out. You're in the FBI. I got my doctorate."

His jaw flexed, and he instantly wanted the vulnerable Macy back. The one who was opening up. Who wasn't afraid to show weakness or admit to feeling hurt. "We could have made it work. Even after you lost the baby, we could have still gotten married. We could have started a family, even if people told us we were foolish because we were young."

"I couldn't let you give up your dreams for me."

"I didn't ask you to. It would have been my choice."

"Besides, I knew if you went into the FBI, you

wouldn't have had time for a family," she continued. "You'd be married to your career. It's to be expected."

"That's an assumption. Not everyone is a workaholic like your father."

She drew in a deep breath and stood, her eyes welling with tears. "But that's all water under the bridge now, isn't it? We can't change the past."

"Macy—"

She took a step away, trails of moisture running down her cheeks. "If you'll excuse me, I need to go lie down now. I'm exhausted."

Before Tanner could convince her to stay and finish this conversation, she fled to her bedroom and closed the door.

He sat on the couch, stunned for a moment. How could Pruett have told Macy that Tanner was relieved they'd lost the baby? Then Tanner knew.

Pruett had always seemed overly interested in Macy. He'd used the situation to his advantage, probably hoping they would break up and that he could make a move. He most likely hadn't counted on Macy moving to Oklahoma and ruining his chances.

Tanner took his hat off and raked a hand through his hair. He and Macy had an undeniable connection back then. How could she have doubted how much he loved her? It wasn't just about their baby. It was about their future together.

Tanner knew that Macy's dad had been married to his work. He'd appeared resentful that he'd had to take care of his younger daughter after her mom died. Of course Macy might have transferred those feelings onto Tanner and think every man was like that.

Tanner had grown up in a home with a mom and dad who loved each other even after thirty years of marriage. They'd been a great example to him of what that kind of union should look like. Maybe that was why he'd remained hopeful while Macy was a skeptic. Their pasts had shaped their view of the future, for better or worse.

Tanner ran a hand over his face, wishing he could turn back time. But the damage had already been done, and it very well could be irreparable.

Macy was still reeling from her conversation with Tanner when she woke up the next morning. She didn't even bother to get out of bed. No, she simply pulled herself up and readjusted her pillows behind her. Then she closed her eyes, wishing she could transport herself from this situation.

On the one hand, it had been such a relief to

finally have that talk. On the other, Tanner had made it seem like what Pruett had told her all those years ago wasn't true, that the man had planted doubt in her head for some reason or another.

Macy clearly remembered that exchange with the fresh-faced cop. She'd been walking to her car after class, still trying to come to terms with losing the baby. Pruett had run into her and struck up a conversation.

The man had always been arrogant, with a touch of mischief in his eyes.

"Tanner told me the news," Pruett had said, falling in step beside her.

"Did he?" Macy blinked with surprise. She hadn't realized the two were that close that Tanner would tell him such intimate details about their relationship. He hadn't exactly hung around Tanner, but they'd been in boot camp together.

"Yeah, I'm sorry about the baby."

She'd paused there in the parking lot beside her car, feeling self-conscious. Getting pregnant had never been a part of her plan. Even though she and Tanner hadn't turned to God yet, she'd wanted to be married first. But losing the baby… Macy definitely hadn't been prepared for that.

"Thanks…we're dealing with it." Her hand had instinctively reached for her stomach.

"Yeah, that's what Tanner said. That it might be a blessing in disguise."

Pruett's words made her pause. "Did he say that?"

"Something like that," Pruett said. "Well, as I'm sure he told you, he just got accepted into the FBI Academy. He turned it down, though. Said you needed him."

The colored had drained from Macy's face at his announcement. "He did? Tanner didn't tell me."

Pruett shrugged it off. "He probably doesn't want to make you feel bad. Sorry to be the one to break the news to you."

A horrible, sickly feeling had washed over Macy. The fact that Tanner hadn't told her said a lot. "I see."

Pruett frowned as if apologetic, even though the emotion didn't quite reach his green eyes. "Maybe I shouldn't have said anything."

"No, I'm glad you did. I don't want Tanner to miss out on something because of me."

"I know it would be easy for resentment to build up," Pruett said.

Resentment? Yes. Macy couldn't go into a marriage knowing she'd stopped Tanner from reaching his dreams. "Yes, you're totally right."

Back in the present, Macy pushed away the thoughts, having no desire to relive that time in her life. Against her desires and maybe even her good sense, she felt conflicted about the past, about the future, and about everything in between.

Macy closed her eyes. She wasn't sure how to react to Tanner when she saw him again this morning. Because now, after finally talking to him, she couldn't help but wonder if she'd made a mistake five years ago. Her head pounded at the thought.

When Addie woke up a few minutes later, Macy knew she couldn't hide out any longer. She needed to use the kitchen to prepare a bottle for a hungry Addie.

She quickly got dressed before gathering the baby into her arms and emerging from her bedroom. She tried to slip into the kitchen unnoticed when she heard someone call out behind her.

"Morning," Tanner said.

She gasped, not expecting to see him sitting on the couch with a newspaper in his hands. "Morning."

"Didn't mean to scare you."

"I was just…" She decided it was better not to deny it. "Yeah, actually, you did scare me."

"My apologies." He folded his paper, stood, and held something out to her. "I thought you might need this."

She stared at the baby bottle in his hands. "You fixed Addie something to eat?"

"I heard her wake up and I know how she gets

when she's hungry. I figured the less time she had to wait, the better."

"Smart thinking. Thank you." She took the bottle, hating how nervous she suddenly felt. She sat on the end of the couch and offered the bottle to Addie. The baby hungrily devoured her breakfast.

She smiled as she looked down at Addie's face. The baby girl was just perfect, Macy realized, from her curly dark hair to her infectious grin. At the end of this, Macy just might have her heart broken again when Addie moved on. She didn't even want to think about it.

Tanner sat at the other end of the couch, looking surprisingly at ease. "How'd you sleep?"

"As to be expected," she said. "I just keep having nightmares about this entire situation."

"I understand. I'm sorry you were pulled into it."

"Stop apologizing. It's not your fault."

"I know. But I still wish you didn't have to go through this. I realize how unnerving it can be."

"Certainly you're not unnerved?"

He shrugged. "Every once in a while, even I feel unsettled."

"Well, at least that makes you human. In case there were any doubts." She said the words lightheartedly, but he'd always seemed a bit like a superhero to her, like he could handle anything.

Even their breakup. She'd known Tanner

would be just fine. He had an inner strength that was admirable. That inner strength was even more noticeable now that he was a Christian because the power wasn't coming from himself. No, it was coming from his faith in a Higher Power. "Devin got back to me this morning about those women we looked into who could be Addie's mom." Tanner shifted the subject and looked notably more serious with his darkened gaze.

Macy felt herself stiffen with anticipation. "Okay. And?"

"The woman who was killed in the car accident has been identified. Her name was… Sarah Lewis." He pulled something up on his phone. "This is her picture. Ever seen her before?"

Macy stared at the picture. It only took her a moment to recognize the woman there. She pulled in a deep breath, and her eyes widened as realization hit her.

"Yes, actually, I do know her," Macy said. "I know exactly who Sarah Lewis is."

FIFTEEN

Tanner watched as Macy swung her head back and forth in disbelief. She continued to feed Addie, but she appeared slightly shell-shocked as she did so. She recognized the woman in the photograph. Could she be Addie's mom? Maybe they finally had a viable lead.

"Tell me what you know about Sarah Lewis," he said, angling himself toward her.

Macy licked her lips and looked in the distance as if gathering her thoughts. "She was one of my clients in Oklahoma."

Tanner jammed his eyebrows together in confusion. "I thought you only worked with kids."

She shifted Addie to her other arm. "I did. Mostly. But I volunteered one night a week doing therapy for parolees."

Tanner blanched at her unexpected announcement. "Did you? I had no idea."

Macy nodded. "I only did it for a year or so, and then I had to step back because my hours at work changed. Sarah was one of my clients. She had to have therapy as a part of her release from prison."

"What was she locked up for?"

"Drug use. She was only behind bars for about eight months, if I remember correctly."

"When did you meet with her? How long ago?"

Macy closed her eyes briefly, as if trying to recall the information. "It was probably a year and a half ago."

Tanner nodded slowly, letting that information sink in. "What else can you tell me about her?"

Macy leaned back, seeming to relax slightly. "She was honestly a sweet girl. She grew up with a single mom. I'm not sure what happened to her dad. But Sarah had had a pretty hard life. Money was tight, and she learned to be street-smart. That's when she turned to drugs and got in with the wrong crowd."

Tanner stored all the information away, thrilled to finally make some headway. It had been a long time coming. "Was she dating anyone?"

Macy nodded after another moment of thought. She looked down at Addie in her arms, still feeding, and frowned. "She was. He wasn't good for her, and I encouraged her to rethink that relationship instead of reconnecting now that she was out of prison."

"Do you remember his name?"

"I think it was Ricky, but I'm not sure," Macy said. "He'd also been in trouble with the law. Like I said, he wasn't a good influence. But Sarah was insecure and felt all alone in the world. It wouldn't surprise me if she went running back to him."

"Anything else?"

She rocked Addie in her arms as the infant came to the end of her bottle. "At her very last session, she said her future was about to change. She didn't expound on it, even when I asked. But I do remember that she'd been looking into who her birth father was."

"We'll look into it."

She paused. "Tanner, do you think she really died in a hit-and-run?"

He bit down a response. He wasn't ready to admit it, but no, he didn't.

In between taking care of Addie, Macy found herself doing what she often did lately: pacing to the windows, looking for any signs of trouble. She hated to think the worst, but whoever these guys were, they'd been a step ahead of the FBI this whole time. She felt like it was only a matter of time before the bad guys located them again.

Even though Tanner had taken precautions, Macy had trouble believing they couldn't be found. Maybe it was paranoia. Maybe it was conditioning. But whatever it was, it had her on edge, just waiting for the next shoe to drop.

As Tanner worked on the computer in the distance, Macy paused by one of the back windows. She thought about what her life should look like right now. On an ordinary day, she would be offering therapy to her clients. In the evening, she would have probably had dinner with some friends from Third Day, and they would have enjoyed some laughs. She would have returned to her house later in the night, had some tea, and gone to bed. It was a simple and predictable life, but also familiar and comforting.

Instead, she was working with her ex-fiancé, taking care of a possibly orphaned baby, on the run, and hiding out. It was like she'd been plopped in the middle of either an action/adventure movie or a nightmare.

Macy closed her eyes and leaned her cheek against the cool window. *Dear Lord, how are we going to get through this?*

And then she knew the answer. Through the grace of God. His strength was the only thing that had gotten her through the tough moments of her life. Losing the baby. Realizing that she and Tanner couldn't be together. Leaving everything she knew behind and going to Oklahoma for the doctoral program there. She hadn't been a believer back then, but she'd turned to Jesus in her desperation, and her life hadn't been the same since then.

Then she'd had the crazy idea to come back here to Houston. To try and reconnect with her father and sister. To face what she'd left behind.

She'd just never thought her journey back home would include Tanner. He was supposed to be married to someone else by now. Out of the picture and out of the question.

Instead, he was just as attractive and kind as he'd always been. And he had that familiar swagger with his boots and cowboy hat. He was her dream guy then and now, and she had no idea what to do about it.

Tanner hung up and called her over to the breakfast bar.

"I can't find any record as to who Sarah's biological father was," he started. "I've been trying to track down any of her acquaintances in Oklahoma. You haven't remembered anything new, have you?"

Macy closed her eyes and tried to recall her sessions with Sarah. She had so many clients that it was hard to keep straight who said what. But...there was one thing that lingered in the back of her mind. It probably wouldn't be much help, but...

"Sarah did mention a friend she'd stayed with when she was going through a hard time. Her name was kind of unique..."

Tanner leaned toward her. "Can you remember it?"

She pressed her eyes together, trying to recall the friend's name. "It reminded me of a fruit. I keep imagining someone dancing with a bowl of oranges on her head." She squeezed the skin between her eyes. "I know it! Clementine. I have no idea about the last name, though. Sarah may have never said it, for that matter."

"That's okay. That's helpful. We can tell Devin and see what he can find."

She crossed her arms and leaned back, hoping the lead would pan out. But she still had other questions. "What about that couple who came in? How do they fit? And who's Michelle Nixon?"

"We're still trying to figure that out."

"You mean the FBI is still trying to figure that out."

Tanner frowned. "That's correct. The FBI and Devin. I asked him to look into things also. I know I can trust him."

"How is the FBI handling all this?" Macy asked softly. "You're supposed to be their foot soldier, yet you're striking out on your own. I'm sure that doesn't bode well. Does it?"

Tanner frowned. "We don't have much of a choice right now but to do things my way, not if we want to keep Addie safe. My job is the least of my worries at the moment. I'll figure that all out when this is over."

The least of his worries? That certainly didn't sound like someone who was married to his career. Could Macy have been wrong all this time?

Before she had the opportunity to think about it, someone knocked at the door.

Tanner rushed to his feet and drew his gun.

"Stay here," he barked.

And Macy knew she had no choice but to listen.

Tanner approached the door slowly and carefully. No one knew they were here. No one but Devin.

Had the bad guys somehow managed to find them again?

Someone pounded at the door again, more urgently this time. "Tanner, it's me. Devin."

Tanner peered out the peephole to confirm it was his friend before opening the door.

"No one followed me." Devin rushed past. "I'm sure."

"Is everything okay?"

"I didn't have your phone number, and I learned something you'll want to hear."

"Then, by all means, have a seat and let's talk." He holstered his gun, trying to relax. But something about the urgency in his friend's voice didn't allow him to do that.

Devin sat on the couch and Tanner perched in

a chair across from him. Macy joined them, anticipation written across her taut features.

Devin rubbed his hands together, his gaze shifting from Macy to Tanner. "We managed to track down Michelle Nixon. I just left from interviewing her."

"What?" Macy's eyes widened as big as the moon. "What did she say? Does she know anything about Addie?"

Devin raised his hand, clearly indicating that Macy needed to slow down. "I'm getting to that. Let me start at the beginning. We tracked Michelle down because of a credit card transaction."

Tanner nodded, listening carefully. Certainly the FBI had discovered this as well. "Is that unusual?"

"She hadn't used it in several days. But, apparently, she ran out of cash. Cash that a woman named Deborah had given her to use, but only if Michelle got out of town."

Tanner leaned forward. "Is this the same Deborah who came into the FBI office?"

Devin nodded, a touch of satisfaction in his gaze. "One and the same. She told me that a stranger approached her and asked her to do a small favor. This woman said she would be paid well, and that it was for a very important cause."

"And Michelle didn't run?" Macy asked. "A stranger approaching with an offer like that should be suspicious within itself. It sounds like a scam."

"Well, at first she was skeptical," Devin said. "But she was also strapped for money. She has a six-month-old, but her name is Bella. She also has a sister named Deborah who lived not far away."

"That's convenient," Tanner said, not liking where this was going.

"This woman who approached Michelle said she was in trouble with her ex-husband, and that she needed to use Michelle's house," Devin said. "She said Michelle should leave town, only use cash so she couldn't be traced, and that she shouldn't come back for at least two weeks."

"But that doesn't make sense." Macy's forehead wrinkled. "Why would this woman need to get out of town because someone else's ex was chasing her?"

"It doesn't at all make any sense," Devin said. "But Michelle was desperate for money, so she agreed to it. I think she figured that some cash was better than none. Unfortunately, she blew a lot of it by buying lottery tickets. That's why she had to use her credit card after all, and that's how we were able to trace her."

"In other words, Deborah, or whatever her real name is, and Mike planned this to a T," Tanner said. "They found a woman with a baby that was Addie's age, who had a sister named Deborah who lived not too far away. That way when the FBI checked out the story, it would seem like it all fell in place."

"That's correct," Devin said. "Deborah even changed her appearance to match that of Michelle's real-life sister."

"Have you reported this to the FBI?" Tanner asked.

Devin nodded. "Saul was there when we questioned the woman."

"Things are finally looking up," Tanner said, glancing at Macy and then back at Devin.

Devin nodded. "Maybe the end is finally in sight."

His words echoed through Tanner's mind. Though his friend was referring to the end of this case, he couldn't help but think about Macy. Was the end in sight—again—for the two of them?

The thought squeezed his gut with regret.

He was going to lose her again, and the sooner he accepted that fact, the better off he would be.

SIXTEEN

"Tanner, I'm worried about Addie," Macy said the next morning. She'd tossed and turned all night, unable to rest because Addie had been fussy and unhappy. "I thought she was just teething, but I think she's getting an ear infection. I know we don't want to take her out into the public, that it's risky. But I'm not sure we can wait. She's warm and she could have a fever."

Tanner gently ran his hand over the top of Addie's head and frowned. "I agree. We don't want her to suffer."

"I know it's dangerous to leave. I don't want to put her in danger. But..."

Tanner's jaw flexed. "If we don't have a choice, we don't have a choice. We'll just take precautions. It's all we can do. I think there's a walk-in clinic the next town over. Why don't you go ahead and pack the diaper bag? We should go soon, before the clinic gets too busy."

Macy nodded and rushed up the stairs. She

quickly put things together, her heart pounding erratically. She was nervous, she realized. More nervous than she thought she would be. But they had to do this, for Addie's sake. All of this was for Addie's sake. Her well-being was Macy's number one priority.

Macy was back downstairs in less than five minutes. Tension pulled across her chest when she saw Addie in Tanner's arms. He bounced her gently, doing a little two-step across the floor. It was such a beautiful sight.

What if that was her baby? Tanner's baby? Things could have been so different... *Jamie.*

Macy hadn't said her baby's name in a while. She hadn't allowed herself to do so. Even saying the name aloud all these years later made a lump form in her throat and tears brim in her eyes.

She and Tanner hadn't known if they were having a girl or a boy, so they'd decided on Jamie, since that would fit both genders. Even though she was only three months along, Macy already had visions of what the baby would be like. First steps. Sleepless nights. First words and smiles and...first everythings. The idea had quickly taken root in her heart.

He kissed Addie's forehead, and her sniffles stopped. The baby rested her head against Tanner's chest.

Macy could hardly stomach it. "Ready to go?"

Tanner nodded and took the diaper bag from

her, wrapping it over his shoulder. "Let's hit the road."

Their sedan was parked in the garage, so they slipped inside without incident. Macy held her breath as Tanner opened the garage door, and they eased out. To her amazement, nothing and no one waited for them outside, either.

Macy had programmed herself to think and expect the worst.

It took twenty minutes to get to the walk-in clinic. When they arrived, the waiting room was already crowded, and full of crying children with runny noses and terrible coughs.

Tanner checked them in, and they took a seat in the corner. Macy continually scanned the others in the waiting room, looking for a sign of someone suspicious. No one caught her eye.

Addie seemed content at the moment, though she'd cried almost the entire way here. She tried to hold her on her lap, but Addie wanted to stand. She straightened her legs and stood on Macy's knees, bouncing happily as Macy held on to her.

A smile stretched across Addie's face when she looked at Macy. The smile widened when her gaze then turned to Tanner.

"I think she's starting to like us," Macy whispered.

"You might be right." He reached out and gently poked her belly, eliciting a giggle from Addie.

"Your little girl is adorable," an elderly woman

beside them said. A ten-year-old boy sat next to her, earphones in his ears and a Game Boy in his hands.

Macy guessed the boy was her grandson.

She started to correct the woman and explain that Addie wasn't hers, but she stopped herself. She just needed to go with it. Saying anything else would only raise suspicions.

"Thank you," she said.

"She's a nice mix of both of you." The woman pushed her glasses up on her nose and glanced back and forth from Tanner to Macy.

"She's sweet like her mom." Tanner winked at Macy.

"Oh, you two are just precious. I have a good sense about these things."

Macy's curiosity spiked, even though she knew it shouldn't. She should just let the woman's comment go. "About what things?"

"Couples who are going to make it," the woman explained. "You two are going to be together until death do you part. I can just tell, and I have a ninety-five-percent success rate."

Macy's cheeks heated. "Is that right?"

Let the woman think whatever she wanted. She and Tanner would not be together forever. They weren't even together now.

"My Johnny and I were together for fifty years, you know," the woman continued.

"That's something to be proud of, quite an accomplishment," Tanner said.

"Accomplishment? I don't know that I'd say that." She chuckled. "It was a lot of hard work. But it paid off in the end. We didn't just give up like couples do nowadays. At the first sign of trouble, they split. That's not the way it was meant to be."

Macy's cheeks warmed even more as she remembered the way things had ended between her and Tanner. "You're right. It's not."

The woman waved her hand in the air. "Anyway, listen to me ramble. I'm sure you have better things to do than hear an old woman blathering."

"No, it's been nice," Macy said. "Thank you."

Just then the nurse called them back. Finally, Macy could flee from this awkward conversation that made her sad and reminded her about what could have been.

Tanner was glad they'd taken the risk of bringing Addie out today. They discovered she had a double car infection. The doctor prescribed an antibiotic, and now Tanner and Macy just had to pick it up. Then they could head back and lie low.

So far, this trip had been surprisingly easy. Tanner hadn't seen any signs of danger. Maybe they'd lost these people who were after them once and for all.

Tanner wanted to believe that, but he was

smarter than to latch on to the idea. He had to remain on guard because trouble could pop up at any minute. That had been proven time and time again.

"Do you want to wait out here?" Tanner asked Macy when they pulled into the parking lot of a big box store.

"There are a few things I'd like to pick up while we're here, things I forgot yesterday. Is it okay if I go inside with you?"

"Of course. We just need to be on guard."

He opened the door for Macy. She slid out and grabbed Addie, who'd just fallen asleep. She left her in the car seat so she could rest.

"Soon we'll have some medicine to make you feel all better," Macy cooed.

Tanner kept an arm around her back as he led them into the store. Inside, it was busy with customers buying groceries, school supplies and other disposables. The crowds could work in their favor and help conceal them.

"We stick together inside," he told Macy, leaning close enough to smell her clean cotton scent and, just for a moment, to relish it.

"Of course." Macy's gaze darted around them.

They dropped off the prescription, and the pharmacy tech told them it would be fifteen minutes until it was ready. That meant they had some time to kill before they got out of here and returned to safety.

Tanner's gaze searched the store as they moved down the aisles while waiting. He didn't see anyone suspicious, but since he wasn't sure what the bad guy looked like, he had to be extra cautious.

He pushed the cart down the aisle of the busy store, waiting patiently as Macy grabbed a few cosmetics and toiletries.

Being out right now with Macy and Addie, in one way, felt way too natural. It seemed like something they'd done countless times before. Like they were a little family, just like the older woman in the waiting room had assumed they were.

He shoved the feeling down. He couldn't go there. They weren't a family, and they never would be. He'd be wise to keep that in mind.

Someone yelped on the other side of the aisle. Tanner's muscles tightened, and he exchanged a look with Macy.

He quickened his steps and peered around the corner. A man in a wheelchair had taken a tumble and now lay sprawled on the floor in the center of the aisle.

"I can't get up," he muttered. "I slipped."

Tanner rushed toward the man, slid an arm under his shoulders, and carefully helped the man back into his wheelchair.

"You're a real lifesaver," he said. "I'm glad you just happened to be close by."

"It's no problem," Tanner said. "Do I need to call a doctor for you?"

He shook his head. "No, I think I'll be okay. But thank you, young man."

Tanner turned back to Macy and Addie, whom he'd left right behind him. But when he looked around, they were gone.

SEVENTEEN

"I'll do whatever you say," Macy muttered as she walked stiffly toward the exit. "Just don't hurt Addie."

The man behind her shoved the gun harder into her back. "Oh, don't worry. I have no intention of hurting the child. We need her."

What did that mean?

The man had appeared out of nowhere. Macy hadn't even seen his face. One minute, she'd been standing there watching Tanner help the gentleman back into his wheelchair. The next moment, something pressed into her side, and she was pulled away.

No one had to tell her the man was holding a gun. She instinctively knew. She also sensed he was wearing a large coat that concealed the weapon. No one else would suspect anything.

As her fight-or-flight response kicked in, Macy had decided she had to be compliant. But what if that was the wrong decision? She didn't know and would have to trust her gut. She had no other choice.

Macy felt rigid as she walked. Her mind raced. What should she do? Most likely, the best thing to do was just to be acquiescent. On the other hand, she'd read the statistics about what happened if you got into the car with someone. You were less likely to ever be seen again alive.

Tanner...where are you? What am I supposed to do?

All it had taken was a few seconds for this man to find her and grab her. Now he led her out the store with Addie snuggled in her car seat.

Maybe Macy could make a run for it in the parking lot.

But as they stepped outside, Macy's stomach sank. A car pulled up at the entrance of the store. The back door opened.

Before Macy could stop the forward motion of events, the man shoved her and Addie into the back, and the driver squealed off.

Macy looked back just in time to see Tanner run out from the store.

Was it too late for him to reach them? Her heart pounded uncontrollably when she realized the answer. Yes, it was too late.

Working quickly, she strapped the seat belt across Addie's car seat, desperate to protect the baby from whatever storm would soon be bearing down on them. She had to keep the child safe.

Work with what you've got in front of you, Macy.

She placed her hand on Addie's chest, trying to keep the baby calm, and glanced into the front seat. A woman sat there. Was that... Deborah? The supposed aunt to little baby Addie? No longer was her hair auburn and neat. No, now it was short and blond.

A man sat beside her. Where Deborah was cultured and elegant, this man looked like a hired gun with his battered jeans, faded shirt and untrimmed hair.

She shivered. Macy wouldn't easily forget the barrel that was still aimed at her. Addie might be "safe" here, but Macy wasn't.

"Where are you taking us?" Macy asked.

"You'll see," Deborah—whatever her real name was—said.

"Why are you doing this?"

"That's none of your business. But Addie is our relative, not yours. You're the one who should be charged with kidnapping. You wouldn't give that precious baby back to us, and you've caused unnecessary trauma to her."

"If she's so precious to you, why haven't you even looked at her since we've been in the car? You haven't asked how she's doing even," Macy said. "She has a double ear infection. We were picking up some medicine for her. Medicine she needs to get healthy. What are you going to do about that?"

"Shut up!" Deborah shouted. "We'll figure things out. We always do. We just need to get back to the lake house first."

At the woman's loud voice, Addie burst into tears. Macy rubbed her hands in circles over the baby's belly, trying to keep her calm before things escalated out of control. "It's okay, sweetheart. It's okay."

"Stop talking to her like she belongs to you," Deborah snapped.

"I'm just trying to make her feel better."

"I'll do that," the woman growled. "As soon as we get somewhere I can take her from you. I've got to make sure your boyfriend isn't following us first."

"You're putting Addie's life in danger," Macy said. "I don't know how you can claim to love her and then put her in this situation."

"I never said I loved her." The woman threw a malevolent grin toward Macy. "I love what she can do for us."

"What does that mean?"

"It's not important." Deborah nodded at the man beside Macy.

The next instant, the butt of his gun came down on Macy's head, and everything went black.

* * *

Tanner pulled his sedan off the side of the road and hit his palms against the steering wheel. He'd lost them. He'd *lost* Macy and Addie.

He rubbed his temples.

Think, Tanner. Think. There's got to be a way to find them.

How could he have let them slip away like that? Had the elderly man been a plant, only meant to distract him? He didn't think so. But these guys had obviously been looking for an opportunity to swoop in, and they'd seized it.

At this point, Tanner had no choice but to call this in. He still didn't know who he could trust at the FBI field office, but it didn't matter now. Those men had Addie and Macy.

"Saul, it's me," Tanner started. "I wasn't entirely honest with you earlier. The truth is that I think someone at the FBI is a mole. I don't know who."

"What?" His boss's voice tightened. "Why would you say that?"

"It's the only way to explain how these guys keep finding us. I don't want to believe it, either, but nothing else makes sense. But listen, that's not why I'm calling."

"What's going on?"

"Someone grabbed Macy and Addie," he said.

"What? I thought that's why you went rogue? To stop this from happening."

"We had to take Addie to the doctor. I'm not sure how someone found out and tracked us, but they did. I need an APB out for a car with this license plate." Tanner told Saul the plate number and vehicle description.

"Why should I do this for you?"

"You shouldn't do it for me," Tanner said. "You should do it for this baby. These people couldn't have gotten too far away at this point. We still could catch them."

"Fine. But don't think I'm going to let this drop."

"I understand. After this is over. Please."

Tanner hung up and tried to sort through his thoughts. He'd seen the sedan come in this general direction. But there were multiple ways it could have turned. Too many side streets and neighborhoods were in this area.

Lord, what should I do?

Tanner eased onto the road. He would canvas these streets one by one if that was what he had to do to find them. And he'd pray that the APB would provide some sort of lead that would help him locate Macy and Addie.

Because there was no telling what these guys might do to Macy. They'd shot at his colleagues. Burned down their safe house. Chased them with a baby in the car.

These guys wouldn't blink an eye at harming Macy.

At the mere thought of it, emotions welled up inside Tanner. He and Macy had a lot of water under the bridge. But he'd seen glimpses of the old Macy he knew and loved. And he missed that Macy.

He only wished he could go back and change things. That he could somehow get through to her. That he could have told her back then that Pruett was wrong. Tanner wouldn't have resented her or blamed her for holding him back from his dreams.

Was it too late to tell her that now? To somehow try and convince her to believe him?

He prayed he would get that opportunity.

At that moment, he spotted the burgundy sedan he'd seen at the shopping center. His eyes zeroed in on the license plate.

That was it! He'd found them.

Thank You, Lord.

As the sound of an alarm registered in his mind, the truth hit him. His eyes moved from the sedan to what surrounded it.

Red flashing lights. A crossbuck. A gate.

He sucked in a deep breath. But someone had left the vehicle on a train track…and a train was headed right toward it.

A loud noise rousted Macy. She sat up and tried to reach for her head—which pounded furiously—but she couldn't.

Her hands were tied behind her.

At the realization, panic raced through her. She tried to move her legs, but her ankles were also bound.

The loud noise sounded again.

She jerked her head to the left, and her eyes widened.

A train was coming right at her.

She was in the sedan. Where was Addie? Deborah and the other two men with her?

They must have jumped out and climbed into a different vehicle. They'd left her here to die, she realized.

Macy tried to scoot near the door, but she couldn't. Her hands were stuck on something.

She looked behind her, straining to see what held her in place. The rope that bound her hands together was also tied to the seat belt clasp.

Her breath caught. There was no way to get out of this car.

She looked up at the train as it got closer and closer.

She jerked her arms, desperate for the ropes to break or come loose. She had to do something. She couldn't just sit here and wait to die.

She glanced at the train again. The locomotive still charged toward her. If she had to guess, she'd say she had one minute or less until impact, at most. Sweat sprinkled across her forehead.

Oh Lord, please help me.

Just then, she heard someone jiggle the door handle.

She looked behind her.

Tanner! Tanner was here. He'd found her! She'd never been so happy to see the cowboy.

"Open the door," he yelled, pounding on the glass.

"I can't." She moved forward so he could see her hands behind her back.

His gaze darkened. "Stay back!"

She scooted away from the window. Tanner bent down and, when he reemerged, he was holding a rock in his hands. He slammed it into the window, and the glass shattered.

He reached inside and his hand found the lock. He jerked the door open and climbed in beside her.

Sweat poured down Macy's back. She glanced over her shoulders again at the approaching train.

One minute tops, she realized.

They weren't going to make it, were they?

"I'm going to get you out of here." Tanner worked with the ties at her hand.

"You're going to get yourself killed, too." The train was so close, she could not only hear it but she could feel it barreling down the tracks. The air was filled with tension. Certainly, the conductor had seen her by now. But she knew he wouldn't be able to brake in time.

Tanner pulled out a pocket knife and worked the rope behind her.

"I've almost got it," he told her.

She looked at the train once more.

It was mere feet away.

There was no way she was getting out of this alive. No way.

EIGHTEEN

With one last burst of strength, Tanner plunged the knife into the rope holding Macy in place. Finally, it snapped.

Not wasting a moment of time, he grabbed her wrist and tugged her out of the car. Moving as quickly as possible, he pulled her off the train tracks and ran alongside the road, toward the train. He knew that once the train hit the car, it could go flying. Anything in its path would be destroyed.

Once they were a safe enough distance away, Tanner paused. His arms went around Macy, and she buried her head in his chest as the sound of metal being crushing against metal filled the air.

He watched as the car bent like a soda can before being spit out farther down the track. Nobody had been there, close enough to get injured.

Thank God.

"Are you okay?" he asked Macy.

She nodded, her head still buried in Tanner's chest. "Yeah, I think so. Tanner, I thought…"

He shushed her and tightened his hold. "Yeah, I know. But you're fine."

"We've got to find Addie. They took her, Tanner!"

He stepped back, needing to look Macy in the eyes. "Who took her?"

"Deborah."

"Her supposed aunt?" His eyebrows pinched together.

Macy nodded. "Yes, the aunt. She had two men with her. I didn't recognize them, but one of them may have been the man who followed us to the barn that day."

"Did they give any hints as to where they were taking her?" Tanner asked.

She hesitated a moment and rubbed the knot on her forehead. "No, none… I don't think so, at least. They knocked me out, so I didn't hear much. What are we going to do, Tanner?"

He glanced around. A couple of cars gathered near the tracks. Sirens wailed in the background. The train was almost at a complete stop halfway down the tracks. The smell of hot, burning metal filled the air.

"First of all, we have to get out of here." Tanner took her arm. "Come on."

He led her to his car, helped her in, and then they took off. Ordinarily, Tanner would try to wait for authorities. But he and Macy would just be wasting valuable time if they did that right now.

He could see that Macy's limbs were still trembling all over. Anyone would be reacting like this in the situation. Tanner knew good and well just how close they'd both come to dying.

He headed back to Devin's old family farmhouse. Everything replayed in his head as the wheels churned against the asphalt. He should have been more careful. He shouldn't have let Macy and Addie out of his sight, not even for a minute.

Finally, he reached the house, pulled into the garage, and put the car in Park. Both he and Macy sat there in silence for a minute, almost as if they both needed to decompress after the events of today.

"You don't think these guys who are after us know we're here?" Macy finally asked, breaking the silence.

"I think they're done with us. They have what they want. *Who* they want. They have Addie."

"So we're no longer a threat." Macy's voice caught with emotion.

"Probably not." He climbed out and took Macy's hand as he led her inside.

He made no apologies about it, either. He couldn't stand the thought of letting her go or of something else happening to her. He'd almost lost her for the second time, and he could barely stomach that thought.

Once they were inside and behind closed doors, Tanner pulled Macy into his arms. To his surprise, she seemed to melt there. She clung to him.

He waited for her to pull away. To object. To reject his touch. She didn't.

"Are you sure you're okay?" he mumbled into her soft hair.

She nodded, moisture welling in her eyes. "I guess. I mean, I'm still shaken. But I'm not really worried about me. I just worry about Addie. Do you have any idea who these people really are, Tanner?"

"No, I don't. But Devin left a message. We have a meeting with Sarah's friend Clementine lined up. You up for the trip?"

Macy stepped back, visibly pulling herself together until a new determination lit her eyes. The sorrow was still there, as was the worry and the sadness. But her underlying strength shone through.

"You know it," she said.

"Great. We'll leave in an hour."

Every time Macy thought about Addie, the sick feeling in her stomach churned harder and harder.

Was the child okay? What if they hurt her? Did Addie miss Macy?

Macy knew she wasn't the child's mom, but she felt so connected with the infant. That little girl needed someone to look out for her. She felt confident that Deborah and her posse were not those people.

Please Lord, help us find her. Keep her safe. Give us wisdom.

She glanced over at Tanner as they headed down the road. They'd only stayed at the farmhouse long enough for Tanner to make some calls. Macy had taken a shower to wash away the grime—to wash away the feeling of the gun against her back—and then she'd had some coffee.

Against all odds, she was glad it was Tanner she was working on with this. She could see his focus in the set of his jaw. She soaked in that handsome cowboy profile, and her heart fluttered.

That was bad news. She knew it was. But the man *had* saved her life. He'd been there throughout this crazy ordeal when it would have been easy to turn this case over to someone else.

"What are you thinking about?" Tanner's voice broke the silence of the car ride.

She dared not tell him the whole truth—that she'd been thinking about him. Remembering what it was like to run her hand through his light brown hair. To touch that strong jaw. To rest in his embrace.

"My thoughts are kind of jumbled right now," she said instead.

"It's a lot to take in." He reached over and grabbed her hand. She didn't object. In fact, she welcomed it. Something about his touch calmed her in a way that defied logic.

She stared out the window at the road as they drove. The sun was setting. She'd always loved Texas sunsets. Today, despite all that had happened, was no different. It reminded her of who was in control, of who ordained their days, and that there was a much Higher Power at play here than what she could comprehend by her own reasoning.

"Where are we meeting Clementine?" she asked.

"At a diner outside of Houston."

Macy glanced at Tanner, uncertain if she'd heard him correctly. "But she lives in Oklahoma."

"I guess she was coming out this way, hoping to find Sarah maybe."

"Does she know about Sarah?" Macy asked quietly.

Tanner nodded solemnly. "Devin told her."

Macy frowned, burdened at the death of the young mom who had so much potential. Sarah had always been pleasant. Confused? Yes. On the wrong path? At times. But she'd had a good enough head on her shoulders to pull through.

Certainly Addie had changed her perspective. Being a mom often did.

Macy recalled their conversations and remembered Sarah telling her once that Macy was a godsend. The girl had needed someone in her life. Macy had done what she could. Maybe she should have done more, but there had been professional boundaries in place.

"Maybe Clementine can help us make some sense of this," Macy finally said.

"We can only hope."

They pulled up to a restaurant ten minutes later. The place was a dive—a dinky one-story building on the side of the highway with a crooked sign reading Val's outside.

Devin was waiting against the wall for them.

"You two doing okay?" he asked, his gaze darting back and forth between the two of them. "You look shaken."

"As well as can be expected," Tanner said, sauntering up to him.

Devin nodded slowly. "The police are looking for you two, you know. Something about leaving the scene of a crime earlier."

"That would be the train crash," Tanner said.

"Yeah, that sounds about right," Devin said. "I'd ask what happened, but maybe it's better if I don't know. That way I can plead ignorance."

"Probably." Tanner shifted and glanced at the window. "Is she here?"

Devin nodded at the door behind him. "She's waiting inside for you to talk with her. She looks scared."

"Anyone else know we're here?" Tanner asked.

"Not as far as I know."

"Okay, we'd better get busy then." Tanner led Macy inside.

"I'll keep an eye on things out here," Devin said.

The scent of greasy, fried food hit her when they walked in. Music from the sixties played overhead. Booths lined the front wall and a row of seats along an eating bar stretched on the other side. A black-and-white-checkered floor was sticky beneath her feet. There were probably ten patrons inside. A few glanced at Tanner and Macy, but most simply ate and continued their conversations.

Macy's eyes searched the restaurant until she saw a girl in the corner, probably in her early twenties. The woman nervously pushed a lock of auburn hair back from her face and glanced around.

That had to be Clementine. Tanner seemed to read Macy's thoughts, and he led her over to the table. Tension built with each step.

"Clementine?" Tanner asked.

The girl nodded, her hands trembling and her eyes wide circles of fear. "That's me."

Macy and Tanner slipped in across from her.

"Thanks for meeting us," Tanner said.

"Did I have much of a choice?"

"You always have a choice," Tanner said. "Can I get you something to eat?"

She nodded, and Tanner signaled the waitress. Clementine ordered a cheeseburger and fries. Tanner ordered sandwiches and fries for him and Macy, as well as drinks. They needed to eat, and the act of everyone sharing a meal together might put Clementine more at ease.

"What brought you out this way?" Tanner asked.

Clementine stared at the soda in front of her. "I had to get away from Oklahoma. I knew it was just a matter of time before I ended up dead. I didn't know what else to do."

"Why is that?" Macy asked. She suddenly didn't care about her own drink.

"Because I know too much. Too much about Sarah. Enough that people would kill me first and ask questions later." She nervously glanced out the window.

Tanner leaned closer. "Have you been threatened?"

Clementine's gaze went back down to the table. "Someone broke into my house back in Oklahoma."

Macy's pulse spiked. "What happened?"

Clementine continued to study the cup of soda in front of her. "I wasn't there. They ransacked the place and left their message very loud and clear they were looking for Sarah."

"Who's they?"

"Sarah's half sister."

"You're sure?"

"I'm positive. I got there as they were leaving and saw them. I hid behind some bushes so they wouldn't see me. But I clearly recognized the woman. We had a couple of run-ins before when I was with Sarah."

"You said they left their message loud and clear," Macy said. "What does that mean?"

"When I wasn't at home, I got an email. It was from someone who claimed to be an attorney. They were trying to contact Sarah. But I could tell it wasn't real. I knew what the lawyer's name was."

Tanner lowered his voice. "Why does someone want Sarah's baby, Clementine?"

Clementine's gaze finally met theirs. "Because she's worth millions."

Tanner stared at Clementine, trying to surmise the truth in her words. Sarah hadn't struck him as the wealthy type. Most drug-using parolees weren't. However, Clementine looked convinced that her words were the truth.

The waitress delivered their food, and Tanner waited until she'd walked away to ask his next question.

"Why would you say that, Clementine?" he asked. "That's the first I've heard of that possibility. Please tell us more."

The young woman sighed and glanced around the restaurant before her eyes met Tanner's again. "It's a long, twisted tale. You sure you're ready for it?"

"As ready as we'll ever be," Tanner said.

Clementine leaned forward. "So, after Sarah was released from prison, she started researching who her birth father might be. She wanted to turn over a new leaf and maybe connect with her family. Her mom died when she was younger, so she was pretty much alone in the world."

"Okay…" Tanner said. He knew that much from talking with Macy.

"She found some of her mom's old papers and went through them. Long story short, she discovered that her dad was Lionel Richardson." Clementine's words hung in the air.

"The oil tycoon?" Tanner finally said. She couldn't be talking about the same person. Lionel was known throughout the area for his wealth and his generosity in donating to charities.

Clementine nodded. "The one and only."

"What… How…?" Tanner started.

"It's true. Sarah didn't believe it at first, either. But she had evidence."

"What kind of evidence?" Tanner asked.

"She'd found some pictures of her mother with

Lionel," Clementine said. "She also found some old journals which mentioned him by name. Apparently, her mom never told Lionel that Sarah was born. She didn't want him to think she was after his money."

"What did Lionel say when Sarah told him this?"

"He didn't believe her. It didn't surprise me. I'm sure many people came forward and claimed to be a relative since Lionel was so wealthy. Sarah asked for a DNA test. She didn't think he would do it, though she did send off her own sample. She eventually gave up."

"What about Addie?" Macy asked.

"Well, a few months after that, she found out she was pregnant."

"What happened to the baby's father?" Macy asked, picking up a French fry and twirling it between her fingers. "Is he still in the picture?"

Clementine shook her head. "He was a drug addict. He overdosed before Addie was born. He was trouble anyway and would have been a terrible father. Either way, he's out of the picture."

"So, how did Sarah reconnect with Lionel?" Tanner asked. "You said he didn't believe her."

"Apparently, he decided to check out her DNA test after all, and he realized that Sarah really was his daughter." Clementine took a bite of her burger and wiped her lips before continuing. "When Addie was born, he had a change of heart. No grandchild of his was going to be homeless. He agreed to meet with her, and he confirmed that he'd once been with her mom."

"How did he react to Addie?" Macy asked.

"He was over the moon. He asked Sarah and Addie to move in, and he wanted to take care of his only grandchild. Of course, he was older—in his early eighties and he'd been diagnosed with cancer. Sarah knew he didn't have much longer, but she was happy to connect with him."

"What happened next?" Tanner asked.

"They had a great relationship," Clementine continued. "Sarah was the happiest I'd seen her in a while. For the first time in a long time, she didn't have to worry where her next meal was coming from or where she would sleep at night. She loved feeling like she finally had a place to belong. Like she had a real family. She got her life back on track."

"What happened?" Macy asked.

Clementine let out a sad sigh. "Lionel died. Sarah was prepared to go on her merry way, feeling blessed that she was able to meet him before he passed away."

"And then?" Tanner grabbed a French fry and took a bite.

Clementine picked at the sesame top of her hamburger bun. "And then the will was read, and almost everything—the majority of Lionel's wealth and assets—were left to Sarah and Addie."

Tanner's eyebrows shot up. Everything was suddenly making sense. Maybe money was the root of all evil…and the source of all the danger that surrounded them.

NINETEEN

"And that's why Addie is worth so much," Tanner muttered. He leaned back in the seat and ran a hand over his jaw.

Clementine nodded, some of her anxiety seemingly replaced with passion. "But there's more than that. You see, Lionel has another daughter, and she wasn't happy to learn she hardly got anything after her father's death."

"Did anyone ever say why Sarah got almost everything?" Macy asked.

"I guess his daughter was pretty entitled. And she never gave her father very much attention. She used him for his money so he didn't feel like she deserved anything. That's what Sarah said, at least. And from what I saw the few times I met her, Sarah was right. The woman was never anything but abrasive."

"What was her name?"

"Robin Brooks."

"Did she look like this?" Tanner pulled up

a picture of Deborah and Mike and showed it to Clementine.

She nodded as soon as she saw the pictures. "That's Robin and her boyfriend Sam. How'd you know?"

Tanner frowned, not liking where this was going. "They're posing as Addie's aunt and uncle. I suppose that officially they are her aunt and uncle, but they're using assumed identities and they said Addie's mom was someone named Michelle Nixon."

"It doesn't surprise me she'd go to so much trouble to get to Sarah and Addie," Clementine said. "She greatly resented Sarah for coming back into her father's life."

"So are you saying that Lionel's daughter is trying to get her hands on Addie so she'll be able to claim her fortune?" Macy's gaze was intense on Clementine.

"That's exactly what I'm saying," Clementine said. "Addie will inherit everything if Sarah dies. It would be easier to control the money through Addie than Sarah."

"That's why Sarah came running to Texas," Macy muttered.

"She knew she was as good as dead if she stayed in Oklahoma," Clementine said. "She headed toward Houston in hopes of finding some psychologist she'd worked with."

Macy stiffened. "Dr. Mills?"

"Yes, she's the one." She stared at Macy, realization rolling over her face. "Is that you?"

Macy nodded, guilt staining her gaze. "Yes, it is."

"She said you were the most trustworthy person she knew. She tried to see you again, but she found out that you'd moved. Your old office wouldn't tell her where, but she hopped online and found a new listing for you."

"We only worked together a few times at the psychotherapy center."

"Well, apparently, you made an impression. Granted, she didn't have that many people in her life she could rely on."

"How about you?" Macy asked, lacing her fingers together like a therapist might.

"I wanted to be there for her, but I'm also trying to clean up my life." Clementine sniffed and touched her silver nose ring. "I'm working three jobs and trying to stay away from the bad influences. I wasn't a good person to rely on."

"Yet you came all the way out here to try and find her," Tanner said, trying to make sense of things.

"After I realized that Robin and Sam would go as far as to try and harm me to get information on where Sarah was, I knew I didn't have much to lose." Clementine pushed the rest of her food away. "I couldn't stay around there or I'd end up dead. Sarah wasn't answering her phone, so I got worried. I decided to try and track you down, Dr. Mills. I even went to the therapy center where you worked. They said you'd taken a leave of absence."

"Sarah never made it to see me," Macy said. "Maybe she was on her way but realized she was in danger. Instead, she stopped by the FBI office and dropped Addie off."

"At least Addie is okay," Clementine said.

Macy frowned. "Clementine, I hate to tell you this, but I was attacked earlier today. Deborah...or I guess I should say Robin... Robin took Addie."

Clementine gasped and hung her head low. "We don't think she'll hurt the child," Tanner said.

Clementine frowned. "No, not yet. Not until they get the inheritance they think belongs to them."

Macy climbed into the car, her head pounding as she processed everything they'd just learned.

"At least we have some answers now," Macy said to Tanner as he sat beside her and pulled on his seat belt. "But what do we do with the information? How do we track down these people?"

Tanner let out a long breath and stared out the front windshield. "Now that we know their names, I'm going to tell Saul what's going on.

He can help track them down—if they haven't tried to go off grid."

They'd already updated Devin, who was escorting Clementine somewhere safe for the evening. The young woman could prove to be a valuable witness when this was all over.

"How do you know Saul can be trusted?" Macy asked. Everyone seemed an accomplice at this point.

"I've known Saul for a while. I can testify to his character." Tanner cranked the engine but made no attempt to move.

At least here in the car they had some privacy, Macy mused. Maybe they both needed a moment to collect their thoughts. They had a lot to process.

Macy reflected on the details Clementine had given them. "You said so yourself that someone at the office is in on it with these guys. How? How did Robin and Sam manage to turn an FBI agent to do their dirty work?"

"Lionel was a wealthy man. If they had even two percent of his income, then they're pretty well off. I'm sure there are FBI agents who can be bought, especially considering what our salary is compared to other professions."

"I don't like the thought of that."

"Neither do I."

"What else do you know about Lionel?" Macy asked.

Tanner let out a long breath. "Besides being wealthy, he was a womanizer, though I heard he mellowed out with age. He always chased women who were younger, who were more like trophies than love interests. I do believe he settled down once and was married for maybe ten years or so."

"Clementine said he died of cancer. Do you think..." She paused midthought. "Is it possible he could have been murdered?"

"Not from what I've heard. I'm sure if there was any sign of foul play concerning his death, the authorities would be all over that."

"There's got to be a way we can track down where they've taken Addie," Macy said.

"You're right. We've got to figure out what that way is." He glanced at his watch. "I think the best thing we can do right now is to get some rest. In the morning, maybe we'll have some other ideas."

"Back to the farm house?"

He nodded. "Back to the farm house."

The ride was silent on the way there. Macy had too many things on her mind. She had no idea she'd made such an impression on Sarah. And to think that Macy hadn't even been able to remember who Sarah was when it counted.

"What are you thinking about?" Tanner asked.

"I'm wondering how things might be different if I'd reached out to Sarah more," she said. Guilt pounded on her.

"You couldn't have known."

She looked down at her lap. "I know. But still…there's nothing sadder than someone who's utterly alone with no one to turn to. I could have been there for her."

He squeezed her hand. "Don't beat yourself up."

But it was going to be hard not to do that. It was her profession to help people, and right now she felt like she'd majorly failed in that area.

Finally, they pulled into the garage at the farmhouse. Tanner checked the place out before calling Macy inside.

"Can I fix you some coffee?" Tanner asked, pausing in the kitchen.

"Sure." Macy sat on the couch, drawing her legs beneath her and pulling a throw over her legs.

A moment later, Tanner set a mug down beside her and then lowered himself on the couch.

"I hope Addie is okay, Tanner," she said, her voice on the verge of breaking.

Even though she'd only been around the child for a few days, she continually found herself thinking about the baby. She wanted to check on her. See if her diaper needed to be changed. To know how her ear infection was doing. Macy just wanted to take the child into her arms and cuddle with her and let her know that she was loved. That everything would be okay. That she would take care of her.

Yet Macy's arms were empty and a good-sized pocket of her heart felt barren.

Tanner reached for her and pulled her into his embrace. She expected herself to resist. But she didn't. She didn't want to.

"I'm sorry, Macy," he whispered over the top of her head.

"Why are you sorry?"

"I'm sorry you believed my career was ever more important than you. That you thought I might only marry you out of obligation. There are so many things I wish I could have done differently."

Macy pulled back just enough to look up at him. She needed to see his eyes, to observe the sincerity there. "Me, too, Tanner. I wasn't thinking straight after I lost the baby. You seemed to be taking everything in stride, and I didn't feel like you understood what I was going through."

He stiffened. "I was trying to be strong for you."

"And I didn't want you to give up the FBI Academy for me."

He tilted her chin up until their eyes met. "I wanted to be with you, Macy."

She rubbed her arms, thinking about how life had played out, how she could have avoided a lot of heartache. "And if you had given up your chance to be in the FBI, you might not be in this position now."

"Maybe things would have taken a different path, but that doesn't mean I wouldn't have eventually made it into the academy again. Things have a way of working out."

Macy lowered her head, her emotions colliding inside her—regret, grief, heartache. "I messed up, didn't I?"

Tanner stroked her cheek. "We all mess up, Macy. I also could have handled things better."

Macy's breath caught as she looked into Tanner's eyes. She instinctively closed her eyes, just like in the old times when they were together. In love.

Stop now, Macy. Stop now.

But she couldn't. And she didn't want to.

All of Macy's nerve endings felt like they were exploding, and she could hardly breathe.

Slowly, their heads came together. Their lips met. Softly and tenderly, yet full of unspoken emotions.

They both pulled away. Macy's heart pounded erratically.

Neither said anything for a moment.

"Are we crazy?" Tanner whispered, his breath hitting her cheek.

Macy ran her fingers over his jaw. "Maybe. But there's never been anyone like you, Tanner.

Even after everything that's happened, there's only been you and no one else."

"I know exactly how you feel. I've held everyone else up to you as the standard. No one else has come close. I've always known you were the one for me."

Their lips met again. She'd missed the way everything else disappeared when they were together. They reluctantly settled back and moved apart.

"At least out of all this ugliness, something good happened," Tanner said.

"That's what I tell my clients all the time. The worst times can end up being the biggest blessings." Macy knew deep inside those words were true, but she'd had trouble believing them at gut level. She'd always thought something was missing, like her worst times were just that—terrible and without redemption. Could that be changing?

Tanner pulled her into his arms. She tucked her head beneath his chin and closed her eyes, feeling content for the first time in a long time.

Emotions clashed inside of Tanner the next morning. On one hand, he felt like he was walking on air. After all these years, he and Macy had truly reconnected and reconciled again. It was like a dream come true. On the other hand, Addie was missing and his career with the FBI was in jeopardy.

As much as he'd like to celebrate, this wasn't the time to do so. There was too much on the line. Right now, he had to concentrate on finding Addie.

He was at the kitchen table drinking coffee when Macy walked out, freshly showered and considerably more bright-eyed than she'd been last night. Yet there was still an underlying heaviness to her gaze. She was worried.

He stood as she came into the room. "Hey, there."

She smiled up at him, almost shyly. "Hey, yourself."

He squeezed her shoulders. "You doing okay?"

"As well as I can, considering Addie is still with those people," she admitted.

"I hardly slept. Too much on my mind."

She frowned and sat down at the table, her sleeves pulled over her hands.

"Can I get you some coffee?" he asked.

"I'd love some."

He walked over to the counter and poured her a cup. Then he grabbed some of the muffins they'd purchased yesterday and put them on the table. Macy would need to eat if they were going to keep up their energy levels.

"Thank you." She wrapped her fingers around the mug. "So...what's up for this evening?"

"We're going to try and find Robin and Sam."

"I remembered something while I was showering," she told him. "I think one of the men in the car said something about a lake house."

Tanner paused. "Really?"

She rubbed her temples. "I mean, I can't be sure. That hit I took on my head made everything hazy. But there's this memory, just right there in my subconscious. I feel like they said something. I know it's not much to go on, but we don't have much to start with, do we?"

"Let's see if we can look up lake houses within a thirty-mile radius. They're too smart to use property they own, but they could have rented something."

"So, you think they could still be in this area?"

Tanner nodded slowly. "I think it's too risky for them to go back to Oklahoma right now. They can't simply return to their normal lives and show up with a baby. It would raise too many eyebrows."

"But if they stay in hiding for too long, they won't get their inheritance."

"That's true also. I don't know what their plan is." He reached for the laptop and typed something. "Well, the lake house may not pan out. There are too many lakes around here."

"Can you narrow it down by how secluded it is?" Macy asked. "I doubt they're going to want to stay anywhere that's too populated. I visualize more of a wooded landscape."

"Good idea." He typed a few more things in

and leaned back. "Well, it does narrow it down some—provided we're on the right track. But there are still a lot of options here."

Macy leaned back and took a sip of coffee. "Did you talk to Devin? Have the police run their credit cards?"

"These guys are obviously paying with cash because the trail has gone cold."

"There's got to be a way to track them down. They have a base of operations in this area. They're too smart to stay at a hotel."

Tanner clicked on a few more links. He saved the most promising houses that fit their criteria as far as distance and seclusion were considered.

"I think we should start making some phone calls," Tanner said. "Let's see which of these are available to rent. That should eliminate some options as they can't lease a house that's already occupied. And this isn't exactly tourist season around here."

"It's better than sitting around doing nothing," Macy said.

Tanner had bought her a disposable phone as well. They divided up the list and began making phone calls. After more than a dozen of them, Macy's eyes lit with excitement.

"I think I may have found a possibility."

TWENTY

Macy pointed to one of the listings on the computer screen. "The owner of this rental said the house has been reserved indefinitely by a nice little family who arrived last week."

"What's the address?" Excitement pounded through Tanner. Could this be it? He could only hope.

Macy told him, and he pulled up the location on the satellite. The property was definitely secluded, surrounded by miles of nothing but woods. There was a large house in the center of the property, and a lake rested beside it. This would cost a pretty penny to rent, but Robin would have the money to pay for it most likely.

"I think this is our best chance," Tanner said, still staring at the screen. "We need to check it out."

Macy jumped to her feet, looking like she was ready to go. "Great. Maybe we can finally find Addie. Maybe she's there."

Tanner bit down, hating to break the news to her. "You should stay here, Macy."

She shook her head, a fire lighting in her eyes. "Take me with you. Please. I can't wait here not doing anything. I can help you find her."

"I don't think that's a good idea." Tanner frowned, not liking the thought of Macy potentially putting herself in the line of fire.

Macy stepped closer to him and lowered her voice. "It *is* a good idea. If Addie's there she'll need someone to take care of her. I can be that person."

She was convincing. Very convincing. Tanner's throat went dry as he looked into her gaze, and he felt his resolve crumbling.

"This could turn ugly." A million worst-case scenarios flipped through his mind. All of them ended with Macy either hurt or dead. The thought caused his gut to clench before a sickening feeling pooled there.

"Please, Tanner." Macy's eyes pleaded with him. She wasn't going to drop this. She felt that strongly about it.

Tanner stared at her a moment, good sense colliding with compassion. He knew how hard it would be for Macy to wait here, not knowing what was happening out there. It would drive her mad as she sat wondering if Addie was okay.

Finally, he nodded and stood. "Okay. You can

come. Just promise me that you'll listen to me. I don't want you getting hurt."

"I'll listen. I promise." Gratitude filled her gaze.

He closed the space between them and pulled her into a long hug, unable to resist her. He was so thankful that despite the circumstances, God had reunited them. But he didn't want to lose her again.

He prayed he didn't regret this. *Please, Lord... watch over us.*

He wished he didn't have to let her go.

"We've got to go," he said, stepping back and planting a quick kiss on her lips. Thoughts of Addie dropped like a rock into his mind. He had to find that little girl. Every moment counted.

Macy straightened. Somewhere in the depths of her gaze, he saw a soldier emerging out of the peace-loving psychologist. "Of course. Let's go."

A few minutes later, Tanner and Macy were heading toward the lake house. Devin was going to meet them close to the location, and Tanner had called Saul to tell him what was going on. He hoped he didn't regret that. Other officers were on standby in case this panned out.

Macy seemed especially quiet beside him. Who wouldn't be in this situation? Things could turn ugly fast. But if they could get Addie back, then the risk would all be worth it. That child didn't deserve to be a pawn in this kind of game. She deserved a loving family who would dote on her and protect her and shower her with love.

He glanced at his GPS to verify their location before pulling to the side of the road. They were a good quarter mile away from the house. This was just where they needed to stop. He found a service road where the sedan would be hidden by trees. In case anyone suspicious drove past, their car would be concealed.

"We go on foot from here," Tanner said, putting the car in Park and turning toward Macy. He still had a lot of reservations about her being here, but he knew he couldn't talk her out of it.

"What about Devin?" Macy asked, running her palms over her jeans.

"He should be here any moment."

She pressed her lips together, a pensive expression on her face and her breathing too shallow. "I hope this goes well, Tanner."

He squeezed her hand, wanting to both reassure her and tell her to stay in the car where she'd be safe. "Me, too."

"Whatever happens, I want you to know how happy I am that we reconnected. I'm so sorry about the way things ended five years ago." Her voice sounded raspy with emotion.

He cupped her cheek, gently stroking his thumb across her skin. "I am, too, Macy, on both counts. We're going to get through this. And, when it's over, I want to see where we go."

A smile stretched across Macy's face. "I'd like that. A lot."

Tires crunched on the gravel behind them. Tanner glanced in the rearview mirror and saw that Devin was here.

They climbed out and met him. He was dressed in tactical gear and looked ready to go. He'd brought bullet-proof vests for Tanner and Macy as well.

"You two ready?" he asked.

"Ready as we'll ever be," Macy said, pulling the vest on and adjusting it.

"Let's head out," Tanner said.

They started their trek through the dark woods. As they traversed through the woodland, Tanner helped Macy over the uneven ground. Finally, they reached the edge of the woods.

In the distance, Tanner saw a house on a lake. The lights were on, and there was one car outside.

Was that Robin and Sam's?

And how exactly were these people planning on claiming this inheritance? Tanner wondered. To do so would require coming forward with Addie, which would lead to their arrest. What exactly did they have up their sleeve?

Tanner didn't like any of this. Robin and Sam

were both conniving and resourceful—and that made for a deadly combination.

Careful to remain hidden, he held up his binoculars. He could see people moving inside. Sam. That was Sam, along with the man they'd seen at the barn after the car chase.

That most likely meant that Addie was in there, too.

"What do you see?" Devin asked.

"Movement." Tanner watched as Sam stepped outside, walking to a SUV with a suitcase in his hand. Of course they'd had to get a new vehicle since their sedan had been crushed by the train. It was obvious that money was no object to them.

"It appears they're packing up to leave," Tanner muttered.

"Are you sure?" Macy asked. "The owner said they were here indefinitely."

Tanner frowned. "Something may have spooked them or someone tipped them off."

"Saul?" Devin asked. "Isn't he the only other person you've told?"

Tanner shook his head. "I don't want to believe that he's our mole. Besides, there are other officers on standby at this point. I hope we don't regret asking them to come as a safety net. But there is one thing I know—if we're going to make a move, we've got to do it soon."

"So what's our next play?" Devin asked.

Tanner narrowed his eyes with thought. "We

have to approach this carefully. We don't want Addie to be harmed. It looks like there are two men. Deborah's probably there with the baby. We've got to go in and take the two men out first. And we've got to be precise and stealthy. Otherwise, we're going to miss this opportunity."

As Devin and Tanner made their way toward the house, Macy lingered behind some underbrush that tickled her ankles and her arms. She tried to remain out of sight, just as she'd promised.

Dear Lord, please protect them. Protect Addie. Help us get out of this whole and healthy and safe.

As she waited, she tried to trust that Tanner and Devin knew what they were doing. Of course they did. They had law enforcement experience. But still her stomach churned. So much could go wrong.

She squinted to see them, but she couldn't from this angle.

She let out a sigh.

This wasn't going to work. She wanted to see what was going on. She *needed* to see.

Making a quick decision, Macy moved deeper into the woods and followed the perimeter of the property. She needed to find a better view, while still remaining out of sight.

She paused halfway around the lake and ducked behind a tree to check out the area.

To her surprise, she saw a second, smaller house nestled out of the way by the lake. Trees covered the top of it so that the building hadn't been visible on the satellite feeds she and Tanner looked at.

Why wasn't this listed on the rental advertisement?

It was probably the owner's house, she realized. It wasn't entirely unusual. Some property owners liked to keep an eye on their rental investments.

Could someone else be staying here instead of at the big house? And, if so, was it the owner or someone else—someone connected with this investigation?

This location seemed even more secluded and safe than the big house. If someone discovered the other hiding spot, this property would allow whoever was staying here the chance to still escape.

If Macy's theory was correct then these people had thought of everything.

Macy needed to get a little closer to confirm her idea. If she was right, she needed to warn Tanner and Devin.

Carefully, she made her way across the thick landscape until she reached the edge of the foliage. Then she ducked down again, waiting to see if anyone appeared.

The lights were on. There was a vehicle parked behind the house. The trunk was open, as if someone was preparing to leave. Just like at the other house.

Macy held her breath, watching and waiting.

Finally, a figure appeared in one of the windows.

It was Robin, Macy realized. As before, she wasn't wearing the neat wig, but she sported short blond hair. And she was holding a baby in her arms. A crying baby.

Addie.

Macy's heart rate surged. Tanner and Devin didn't know about this location. And she couldn't call them to let them know. She couldn't even text them for fear that the buzzing of the phone might alert someone to their presence. She couldn't risk it.

What should she do? She'd promised to remain in the woods and out of sight. But she couldn't let Robin get away.

She watched another moment. There didn't appear to be anyone else in the house with Robin other than Addie. Macy wasn't a fighter, not a physical one at least. But could she take Robin down if she had to?

Making a quick decision, Macy darted toward the house. She didn't stop until she reached the outside wall. Her heart hammered frantically as she pressed herself into the smooth wood siding.

What was she doing?

It didn't matter now. She had come this far. She had to see this through.

She dragged in some ragged breaths and tried to formulate the next step of this plan. But that was the problem—she didn't have a plan.

Her fingers dug into the side of the house, and she paused as a voice drifted out through the window.

"We've got to get back to Oklahoma," Robin said. "As soon as we get the money, then Addie can have an unfortunate accident. We don't need her slowing us down. Her incessant crying is driving me mad. I wish I could get rid of her now."

Macy's heart lodged in her throat. How could someone be that heartless? She couldn't let them get away from here with Addie. Even if Macy had to sacrifice herself. She would do whatever necessary to insure the child's safety.

"Let me go get our stuff," Robin said. "We need to get out of here before they find us. We'll lay low at a new location for a while until this blows over, and then use the cover story we came up with."

Macy had to go solo on this, and that was against everything she wanted to do. She'd never wanted to be the hero. But that was the position she was in now.

"I'm going to put the baby down and grab my stuff," Robin said. "Come over here. Now."

This was Macy's chance. She peered in the window, though barely. She couldn't risk being seen.

There was Addie!

She sat in a portable playpen, tears streaming down her face. That poor baby. She needed her medicine. Her ears must be making her miserable—not to mention the emotional trauma of all this.

Macy stepped out farther, determined to get a better look. As she did, she caught a glimpse of Robin disappearing into a back hallway.

It was now or never.

Macy darted toward the door. She held her breath as she grabbed the handle. *Please let this be unlocked!* She twisted it and, to her surprise, it turned.

She could hardly breathe as she nudged the door open. She slipped inside the house. As she did, Addie cried harder.

Macy froze.

"Stop crying," Robin yelled from the other room. "You can sense I don't like you, can't you? I'll get this over with as soon as I can, you little brat."

Anger burned inside Macy. Robin had no right

to be around a precious child like Addie. In fact, she should be behind bars where she'd never be able to hurt anyone again.

"I can't get everything done with you in my arms," Robin said. "You stay in the playpen. And for the sake of all that's good in this world, please stop crying."

Macy swooped in, afraid she was going to miss her chance. She grabbed Addie and whispered softly in her ear. "It's okay. I'm here."

Addie quieted almost immediately. She looked up at Macy and grabbed at her hair. Her sweet baby scent drifted up to her, momentarily calming Macy's racing heart. Then she whimpered, as if her relief was short lived, and let out some small cries again.

"We've got to get out here," Macy whispered.

With tension stretched across each of her muscles, she started toward the door. That had been easy. A little too easy.

She had to make a run for it.

"I wouldn't do that if I were you," someone said behind her.

Macy froze before slowly turning around. Robin stood in the living room, her entire body poised as if ready to pounce. Hatred gleamed in her eyes as she stared at Macy.

"I should have known you'd find me," Robin said. "You seem like the stubborn type."

"I don't want any trouble," Macy said, taking

a step away from the crazy woman in front of her. "I just want to make sure Addie is okay."

"I'll make sure she's okay," Robin growled, pacing closer. "And I'll make sure I'm okay in the process."

"You can have the money. We can work something out. This situation isn't good for Addie, though. You know that." She had to somehow get through to Robin.

Addie's cries became louder at the sound of Robin's voice and Macy pulled her closer, desperate to calm the child down. The sound was only adding to Robin's agitation.

The good news was that the woman didn't appear to have a gun. At least she and Macy were on equal ground at the moment.

"You were supposed to die," Robin continued, bitterness dripping from her gaze.

Macy held Addie closer. "I must have survived for a reason."

She snorted and raised her hands. "Think what you want. Give me Addie back."

"I can't do that."

"You don't have much of a choice. My guys are headed this way. You might as well make this easier for yourself."

She didn't know about Tanner or Devin yet, Macy realized. At least they had that to their advantage.

"I'm not giving Addie to you." Macy's gaze

wandered her surroundings, looking for something to defend herself with. There was so little here, though.

Until she saw the fireplace. Then an idea hit her.

"Just give me the baby," Robin said, stretching out her arms even farther.

"Over my dead body." As Macy said the words, Addie sniffled.

"That's ridiculous. Give me the baby." Robin reached for her again.

In one quick movement, Macy reached down and grabbed a handful of ashes. She flung them at Robin's face.

Robin reached for her eyes, screeching with pain and fury. Macy knew she had to seize this opportunity. She darted outside, her heart hammering out of control with every step. So many things could still go wrong.

Dear Lord, watch out for us. Please.

Robin's moans and curses came from inside the house. Macy had to get Addie as far away as possible before the woman got a second wind.

She made a beeline toward the woods. Her arms clasped Addie, and she prayed that she'd have steady footing on the uneven landscape.

What were Tanner and Devin doing? If she called for their help, would she only end up getting them killed? Exposing them?

It didn't matter right now. Right now, she had

to run. Her lungs burned as she continued to sprint toward the trees in the distance.

Just a little farther, and the forest would offer some protection.

As soon as she darted behind the trees, she heard a footstep in the distance.

She looked up just as Agent Manning stepped from the darkness.

Tanner and Devin moved closer to the lake house. They had to take out these two guys outside and then get inside to find Addie. One wrong move and their whole plan could be ruined.

He motioned to Devin, and they split up. Tanner moved stealthily toward the man he'd seen driving the car, the one who'd followed him and Macy to the barn. The man heaved another suitcase into the trunk of the vehicle.

These guys were definitely planning on getting out of here. They probably changed locations every few days to avoid being caught.

As Tanner took a step toward him, he heard a moan from the other side of the house. Devin must have reached Sam already.

At the sound, the man in front of Tanner tensed and reached for the gun at his waist.

Tanner had to make his move now.

He lunged at the man and slammed him on the ground. Before the man could react, Tanner brought his fist back and smashed it into the man's jaw.

The man sprang to life and wrestled Tanner off him.

He reached for his gun again, but Tanner kicked it from his hands.

The man sneered and lunged at Tanner.

They both rolled over and popped up to their feet almost at the same time—facing each other and ready for hand-to-hand combat.

"Where's Addie?" Tanner asked, pacing in a half circle and waiting for the man to make his next move.

"Wouldn't you like to know?" The man smiled, but it didn't reach his eyes. He had no respect for human life, and that made him the worst kind of perpetrator to encounter.

"We just want the baby. You can leave as planned, and we won't stop you."

"The plan is to take the baby with us. Nice try, though."

"Who are you anyway?" Tanner asked, his entire body tense and ready for battle. "How are you connected with this?"

His opponent continued to prowl, reminding Tanner of a lion that was about to strike as they faced off. "That's none of your business."

"I'd say it is."

"You're going to have to kill me before you get that baby."

He lunged at Tanner, slamming him into the house behind them. The entire building shook. Tanner felt a jolt of pain before a blinding ache coursed through him.

As the man charged toward him again, Tanner turned. His elbow connected with the man's chest, sending him backward, and knocking the wind out of him.

Tanner tackled the man to the ground again and gave him one more punch to the jaw.

Before the man could get back to his feet, Tanner jerked him up and slapped handcuffs on his wrists. He shoved him against the car before wiping the blood off his lips.

"Now, where's Addie?" Tanner demanded.

"I'll never tell." He sneered and raised his chin.

Devin appeared with Sam in tow from around the side of the house. Sam had a bloody lip and a swelling around his eye.

"He's not talking," Devin said, shoving Sam toward the car.

"Did you check the house?"

"They're not there," Devin said.

Tanner stepped closer to the men. "Tell me where she is."

Sam smiled again, that same evil, sardonic grin. "Now why would I do that?"

Tanner was missing something, and he had to figure out what. Everyone's life depended on him doing that sooner rather than later.

TWENTY-ONE

Macy pulled Addie closer and took a step back. The child clung to Macy, on the verge of tears. The farther away from Manning that Macy stepped, the more she felt like the forest was closing in. The more isolated she became. The farther hope slipped away.

"You got the baby," Manning said.

He appeared all business in his black cargo pants and a matching black T-shirt. She'd guess he had a bulletproof vest beneath it. A gun was strapped to his waist, and he didn't appear the least bit surprised to find her out here.

"I was afraid they were going to get away with her," he continued.

"I was also." Macy's throat felt tight as she said the words. "But I've—we've—got to move. I'm afraid they'll find us."

"Absolutely. You need to get out of here before those guys come after you. I'll accompany you." He reached for her arm to escort her.

Macy's stomach sank. What if Manning was the mole? She didn't like this, but maybe she should play along and not tip him off that she didn't trust him. Hopefully, Tanner and Devin would be back soon and could help in case things turned ugly.

"How'd you find us?" She moved carefully through the woods with Manning's hand on her arm, guiding her.

"I was backup."

"And you're the only one who came?" Something wasn't adding up. Macy tried to take a step away, tried to consider her options. She couldn't outrun the agent, especially not with Addie in her arms. She'd end up injuring both herself and the baby. She couldn't risk that.

"I happened to be close by when Saul called me," Manning said.

Was that because he was in on all of this?

Macy's feeling of despair tried to bite deeper. How was she going to get out of this? If only she could tell Tanner what was going on. She didn't know anything about hand-to-hand combat. But she could use her mind.

"We should keep walking." Manning led her farther away from Tanner and deeper into the middle of the vast forest surrounding the house. "We need to make sure you're out of sight."

The meaning of his words caused ice-cold fear to form in her gut. Her being out of sight would give him the opportunity to kill her and take Addie without anyone being the wiser.

"I think I'll be okay. Why don't you go help Tanner and Devin? I'm worried about them."

"I think they're handling themselves just fine. Besides, Tanner is in a world of trouble with the FBI. He should have never gone rogue."

Macy raised her chin, determined to defend Tanner. "He was looking out for Addie."

"Look how far that got him."

She ignored his comment, deciding to play along and stay on his good side. "When's everyone else going to arrive?"

She stepped over a root, trying to be careful. The ground was uneven out here. It was so hard to see.

"It's hard to say. This place is off the beaten path, to say the least."

Which was why it was weird Manning was here, Macy mused. Had Tanner called him as backup? Or was there more to this story?

"I think we should wait for Tanner and Devin now." She stopped beside a tree, trying to both catch her breath and calm her racing heart. Plus, she needed time to think.

"No, we need to keep moving." Manning's grip on her arm tightened. "We're almost at the road."

"We're more likely to be spotted there," Macy said, resisting the urge to yelp. His grip was painfully tight. Certainly Addie could sense her anxiety, her racing heart. As if to confirm, the baby let out another deep-seated cry.

"You think there are more of these guys than the people you saw at the house?" Manning glanced around, as if looking for approaching trouble.

"I'm sure they have little foot soldiers doing their work," Macy said, knowing she was baiting him. But she had to buy some time. "I guess Robin and Sam had money to hire whoever they wanted. Cowards. They couldn't even do their own dirty work."

Macy glanced at Manning and saw a shadow cross over his face. The bad feeling continued to churn in her gut.

Psychology, Macy. Use psychology. It's what you know best.

"I'm glad there are honorable men like you to stop people like Robin and Sam," she continued.

"That's my job," he said.

She swallowed hard. "I know your parents must be proud of you."

"I suppose."

"Oh, stop being humble. They probably have pictures of you all over their house. Ones of you at the FBI Academy, getting awards and recognition for your service. You're the type of guy who should be a hero."

He said nothing.

"Why'd you want to join the FBI in the first place?" she asked, trying to passively get through to him. They were getting closer and closer to the road, which made Macy's gut twist tighter and tighter.

"To put away the bad guys. Of course."

"Did you always want to be the good guy?"

His grip on her arm tightened, probably subconsciously. "Actually, I did. Who doesn't want to be the hero?"

"The most important thing is protecting the innocent, right?"

The shadow over his face deepened. Just ahead, she could see the highway. Could see the gleam of a vehicle.

She knew exactly where this was going.

And she couldn't let that happen.

She paused beside a tree, her head pounding with anxiety.

"Why'd you stop again?" Manning asked, trying to nudge her forward. "We're almost there."

Manning was going to take Addie and leave Macy for dead. She had no doubt about that.

"I'm not going anywhere else without Tanner. I promised I'd wait for him."

"He told me to come get you."

"But he didn't know where I was." Her voice cracked as she said the words.

This was the moment when Manning would

either offer a logical explanation for his presence or show his true colors.

Macy could hardly breathe as she waited for his reaction.

Had her talk done any good? Had it made him realize that he was wrong to do this?

She looked up and saw Manning's placid expression turn into a sneer. "You think your little boyfriend's a hero, don't you?"

"I know he is." She'd turned her back on Tanner once. She'd never do that again.

"Well, we'll see if he can get you out of this one. Hand over the baby."

Macy glanced at Manning and saw he was holding a gun.

Macy had been right. He was the mole.

Tanner left Devin at the house with the two men, and he sprinted toward the woods to find Macy. Addie was still missing, as was Robin. A bad feeling churned in his gut.

He reached the edge of the woods and paused. He wanted to call out to her, but he knew better.

Something was amiss here.

Macy wouldn't have left her spot unless something had happened.

Where had she gone?

With his gut still clenched, he paced deeper into the forest, searching for her, fearing the worst.

Had Robin done something to Macy? His anxiety deepened.

Just then, he heard the sound of tires against gravel. Someone was driving this way and moving fast—urgently fast.

He darted toward the noise just in time to see a sedan barreling down the lane toward the county highway in the distance.

Robin, he realized.

Did she have Macy and Addie with her? He tried to glance through the car window, but he couldn't see anything. The glass was tinted, and the car was moving too fast. Besides, Macy could be on the vehicle's floor and out of sight.

He couldn't let Robin get away.

Just as he reached the driveway, the car zoomed past. He could feel the heat from the vehicle, only inches away from him. Another step closer and he would have been sideswiped.

Quickly, he pulled out his gun. Aiming carefully, he pointed his barrel at the tires.

He pulled the trigger and heard a pop.

He'd hit one tire.

But Robin wasn't slowing down. She continued to charge ahead, her car wobbling on the uneven tires.

He raised his gun again, aimed and shot out the other back tire.

Another pop sounded. This time the car veered

out of control. It careened, only stopping when the front bumper collided with a giant oak tree.

He sprinted toward the car, and just as he reached it, Robin pushed her door open and tried to climb out. She'd taken only a step when he grabbed her arm, turned her around and hand-cuffed her.

His gaze shot to the back seat.

It was empty. No Macy or Addie.

"Where are they?" he demanded.

"Who?" She sneered, as if she was enjoying this. The woman looked crazy. Black dirt—or was that ash?—lined her eyes. Her hair stood up in several directions. She smelled like sweat and grime.

"Where's Addie? Macy?"

Her sneer remained. "Wouldn't you like to know?"

He pressed her against the car. "Tell me. Now."

"I'm not making this any easier on you," she muttered.

"Fine. We can do this the hard way." He jerked her away from the car. "I'll let Devin deal with you."

"You do that. Meanwhile, your little girlfriend can suffer."

His muscles went taut. "What do you mean?"

"Nothing. Except that she should have stayed out of it."

He stopped right there on the gravel driveway and jerked Robin around to face him.

"Tell me where she is. Now." His voice came out as a low growl.

He could see the smart remark on the tip of her tongue, so he gripped her arm even harder. "I'm going to make sure they throw the book at you and that you spend the rest of your life in jail."

"You have no pull." The challenge in her gaze taunted him.

"Oh, but I do. You're facing kidnapping and murder charges. No amount of money will buy your way out of this one."

"My inside sources told me you're on the outs with the FBI."

"But my friend Devin is engaged to a federal prosecutor," he bluffed. "I'd say he has some pull."

Her face paled. His ruse had worked.

"We've got evidence," he continued. "Enough to put you away for life. So I suggest you start talking so I can at least tell prosecutors that you were cooperative. Crimes against infants are never taken lightly. And when we tell everyone what you did—how you killed that poor child's mother for money—there's not a single person who will have any compassion for you."

She swallowed hard. "There's a second house on the lake. She's there with Addie."

"That's what I needed to know." He kept his hand on her arm and continued to lead her to Devin.

"I'd hurry. Because she's not there alone."

A bad feeling churned in Tanner's gut.

He followed the woods back to the second house, hoping and praying that Macy and Addie were okay. The door was ajar when he got there.

He drew his gun, preparing himself for the worst.

Carefully, he stepped inside. This was definitely where Addie had been staying. There were baby supplies everywhere. Some kind of dirt was on the floor. Ashes. Those were ashes. Just like Robin had on her eyes.

There's been a fight here, he realized.

Most likely, a fight between Robin and Macy. It had ended with Robin driving away without either Macy or Addie.

So where were they?

At once, the truth hit him.

What if Robin had been leading him astray? Buying more time so someone else could grab Addie?

It didn't all make sense to him. If Robin was locked up for this crime, she wouldn't get the money anyway. But who knew what she was planning. Maybe she simply thought it was the ultimate justice for Addie to end up with nothing and with no one to take care of her. That if she couldn't have her father's money, no one should.

He walked around the outside of the house, searching for any other evidence of where Macy might be. He knelt on the ground outside the window.

There. Foot impressions in the dirt.

Those were Macy's size.

Macy had been here. She must have discovered this house somehow, grabbed Addie and escaped.

But where had she gone?

There was still a mole out there, and if that person got their hands on Macy before Tanner found her, it could spell disaster. He had to find her. Now.

He wandered back through the woods. That was the most likely place Macy would have gone. But, if she was hiding here, why wasn't she emerging?

He didn't like this.

Gun drawn and ears perked, Tanner listened for any telltale sounds.

He used the trees for cover, on guard against anyone else who might be out here, as he moved through the area. Something was going on out here. He just wasn't sure what.

A stick cracked in the distance.

The skin on Tanner's neck pricked.

He knew something too large to be an animal had caused the noise.

Then he heard it. It was Addie. She let out a wail.

Macy was close enough that Tanner could hear Addie. But Macy was remaining quiet. Why?

Something was wrong.

Carefully, Tanner crept forward, certain to be on guard for the unexpected.

"Tanner, watch out!" someone yelled.

Macy. That was Macy.

He ducked behind a tree as a bullet sliced by him, lodging into a tree only inches away.

His adrenaline surged.

Who was with Macy? Who'd fired that shot?

Was it the inside man who'd been feeding information to Robin and Sam the whole time? Anger rushed through him at the thought.

That betrayal didn't matter right now. What mattered was keeping Macy and Addie safe. He'd deal with the rest later.

Carefully, Tanner peered out from around the trunk of a massive oak, trying to identify the shooter.

"Hush, you're making this harder," someone barked. "Can't you keep that baby quiet?"

Tanner recognized the voice, but he didn't want to believe it. It was… Manning.

Manning had been the mole.

How could Tanner not have seen it? The man had been under his nose this whole time.

Another wave of righteous anger swept through him.

If there was one thing worse than a bad guy, it was a bad guy who pretended to be a good guy. Tanner had no mercy for men like that.

"Put the gun down, Manning," Tanner called. "Backup is on the way. This will all be over soon. There's no way out for you."

"Backup isn't on the way. Not anymore," Manning said. "I already called and told them it was a false alarm. You're on your own Tanner. Let's just make this easy, and you can give yourself up."

Was he bluffing about backup? Tanner would guess he wasn't.

Tanner was going to have to handle this on his own.

He darted toward another tree, trying to get a closer look. Another bullet whizzed by.

Addie screamed at the sound.

His breathing quickened. Manning was heartless to terrify a child like this.

He was also shooting to kill. Those bullets were all at heart level.

Tanner peered around the tree trunk and spotted the agent standing in the distance. He gripped Macy's arm and pulled her and Addie in front of him as human shields. In his other hand, he held a gun.

He was just waiting for Tanner to step out. He'd kill him, kill Macy, and then run away with Addie.

He must have been paid a pretty penny to go through all this. And Robin must think the right kind of defense team could get her out of this. Little did she know that money couldn't buy everything.

Just as Addie let out another cry, Tanner saw his opportunity. Manning glanced down at the baby, agitation staining his features— agitation that was growing by the moment.

Tanner raised his gun. Lined up his target.

Lord, direct my aim. Please. Keep Macy and Addie safe.

He double checked once more and then pulled the trigger.

Manning froze momentarily before letting out a moan. A second later, he fell to the ground.

Tanner got him in his neck, the very place where a bulletproof vest wouldn't cover. The shot may not be enough to kill him, but it would put him out of commission until he could get to a hospital.

Tanner rushed toward them and grabbed Manning's gun as the agent writhed in pain on the ground. His hand gripped the bullet wound near his throat, and his eyes bulged.

"I thought more of you," Tanner said, growling down at the agent.

"You wouldn't understand," Manning whispered.

"Why's that?"

"Because you're like a Boy Scout. You always try to do the right thing. As if you're incapable of doing anything but the right thing."

"Better to be a Boy Scout than willing to sell out to the highest bidder. I think the court system will agree with me."

Tanner glanced at Macy, raking his gaze over her for a sign of injury. She and Addie both appeared fine. Thankfully.

Relief washed through him.

He stepped closer and squeezed Macy's arm, resisting the urge to pull her into his arms. There'd be time for that later.

"You're okay?" he confirmed, keeping his voice low.

Macy nodded, her gaze holding a measure of exhaustion and relief. "Yeah, I'm fine. Now I am, at least. I knew you'd come."

"And Addie?" He ran a finger over the child's hand.

Macy looked at the baby in her arms, worry filling her gaze. "We do need that antibiotic. She's burning up."

"I'll get backup here now." He pulled out his phone.

Before he could dial, sirens sounded in the background. Help was on the way.

Maybe all of this was finally over.

Macy put Addie into the crib in her spare bedroom. The baby had fallen into a peaceful slumber after taking a bottle. She was now on antibiotics, and her ear infection should clear up in a few days. The doctor had said that, despite everything that had happened, she would be fine.

Macy had been given permission by Child Protective Services to take care of Addie and bring her into her home. That was in part because a note from Sarah had been found in a recently discovered safety deposit box. She'd instructed that if anything happened to her, Macy was to take care of Addie.

Macy didn't know what to think. She was flattered. Ridden by guilt. But overall, she reminded herself to be grateful.

She didn't know what had compelled Sarah to choose Macy to take care of Addie, but she was thankful for the opportunity. Maybe those therapy sessions they'd done together really had had an impact on Sarah.

Either way, Macy couldn't imagine Addie being with anyone else at this point. The events of the past few days had bonded them quickly and irrevocably.

Someone knocked at the door, and Macy answered it, knowing exactly who was on the other side. She didn't have to live in fear anymore. The bad guys were now behind bars.

Tanner stood on her porch. Wearing his cowboy hat and boots. His hands were still bruised from the fight that had broken out at the lake house. There was a small cut on his cheek and stitches on his forehead.

But he'd never looked so good or appealing.

As soon as Macy saw him, she threw her arms around his neck in a warm hello.

"I could get used to this greeting," he muttered with a smile.

He stepped inside her house and closed the door behind him. He pecked her lips with a quick kiss that lingered on the verge of more.

"How's Addie?" he asked, keeping a hand at Macy's waist.

"She's fine. Just went down for a nap. I think she's feeling better."

Macy reluctantly pulled away from him and paced into her kitchen. She poured him some coffee, anxious to hear his update.

"How'd everything go?" she asked, her voice feeling raw with emotion and anticipation.

"I'm back in good standing with the FBI." Tanner followed her and sat at the breakfast nook.

He already seemed at home here, like he easily fit into her house. Like he belonged here with her and Addie. Macy hoped that might be a reality someday.

"That's great news," she said. "I knew they'd come to their senses when they heard all the details."

"Manning will be going away for a long time." He rested his arms on the table, his hands clutching that mug of coffee.

"I still don't understand how Manning was connected with Robin and Sam." Macy gripped her own coffee mug, concern filling her gut. She couldn't stop thinking about what had happened since that day at the lake house.

"The FBI often hires outside of law enforcement, depending on their need at the moment. Manning went to school and studied finance," Tanner said, taking a sip of his coffee. "So did Sam. They met there, and when Sam decided he needed an inside connection with the bureau, he connected with his old classmate. Apparently, he paid Manning fifty thousand for any information he was willing to feed them about this investigation."

"That's a hefty price tag."

"It sure is. I didn't realize it, but Manning requested this assignment. He said it was because he was mentoring Armstrong. Secretly, he wanted an inside connection to the case, so he could give up information to Sam and Robin and increase his net worth a little in the process."

"Sam and Robin hired other people to do their dirty work, though, right? Not just Manning."

Tanner nodded. "That's correct. They had plenty of money at their disposal, so they hired some local guys. At least one had military training. They fed them a story about Addie being kidnapped to make everything seem more legit."

"How did they find us after Addie's doctor appointment that day? Did you ever find out? I really thought we'd lost them."

"From what I understand they knew the road we traveled down after leaving Devin's," Tanner said. "They kept an eye on that street, knowing that it was the only way out of town. They saw us leaving, and their hunch paid off."

"Clever on their part. But one other thing that still doesn't make any sense to me is how they planned on taking the inheritance after kidnapping Addie."

"They planned on saying that the FBI took Addie illegally. They already had papers for the lawsuit drawn. They'd covered everything. The only thing they didn't anticipate was you."

Macy smiled. "And you. Perhaps they didn't expect an agent to be as dedicated."

"The whole situation was twisted. I'm just glad it's over."

Macy leaned back in her seat, unable to comprehend the lengths people would go through for money. "Just how much did they stand to gain through this?"

"Twenty million."

Macy's eyes widened at the number. "Wow. That's not a small chunk of change."

"No, it's not. People have killed for a lot less."

"They almost got away with it, didn't they?" She swung her head back and forth in disbelief.

Robin and Sam had been close. Only an hour or so away from fleeing from the lake house and hiding somewhere new after Manning tipped them off that there was police activity in the area.

"It's a good thing we found them when we did," Tanner said, almost like he could read her mind. "Otherwise, we may have gotten caught up in a legal battle, and who knows what would have happened to Addie in the process."

Macy lifted a prayer of thanks. "I'm just glad it's all over. Have I said that yet?"

"You can say it as much as you'd like. Things could have turned out a lot differently." Tanner put down his coffee and reached across the table to grab her hand. "As much as I'm sorry all of this happened, I'm incredibly grateful that it brought me back to you, Macy."

She felt herself beaming as she looked up at him. But there was something she needed to say, something that weighed on her like an immovable boulder.

She licked her lips as her eyes met Tanner's. "I know I've said this before, but I'm sorry about the way I handled things five years ago, Tanner. I believed the lies, and I should have talked to you. That was wrong of me."

He squeezed her hand again. "We all make mistakes. I've certainly made my fair share."

Macy stared into Tanner's beautiful, expressive blue eyes. They hadn't really had a chance to talk yet. Not to really talk, at least.

Everything was like a whirlwind after Robin and Sam had been arrested. It had been an endless stream of interviews, doctor's appointments, meeting with attorneys and more.

"So where do we go from here?" Macy asked, holding her breath as she waited for his response. "God made our paths cross again after all these years, and we both finally have some much needed closure."

"I was hoping you might ask where we wanted to go from here." Tanner's eyes crinkled as he smiled.

Macy raised her eyebrows, curious now. "Were you?"

"As a matter of fact, yes." He released her hand and stood. "Because I was hoping we could pick up where we left off before that Dear John letter."

Suddenly, nothing else mattered. Macy wasn't

sure if she'd heard Tanner correctly—or if she'd understood. Her heart stammered in her ears.

"What do you mean?" she asked.

He got down on one knee, just like he had all those years ago. "What I mean is—Macy Mills, will you marry me?"

All the breath left her lungs as she stared down at him. This was her second chance, her opportunity to make things right, to reverse the mistakes she'd made in the past.

"You're serious?" she whispered.

"Of course I'm serious." He held out a diamond ring. The same diamond ring he'd given her five years ago.

Macy would never forget what it looked like, felt like. It was beautiful then, and it was even more beautiful now.

"You saved that?" she asked.

"I did."

She stared at it, unable to speak.

"You're killing me, Macy." Tanner looked up at her, waiting for an answer.

"Yes. Yes. Of course I will!" She threw her arms around him, almost knocking him to the floor in the process.

Tanner chuckled and planted a kiss on her lips. When he pulled away, he slipped the ring on her finger. It fit, like it was always meant for her and her alone.

Macy stared down at it, feeling like all of this was surreal. But this ring was real. Tanner was real.

"Tanner, I just can't believe this," she whispered.

He rested his hands on her waist, making no effort to move away. "Believe it."

She rested her hands on his cheeks, cradling his face and never wanting to look away. "I love you, Tanner. I always have."

He tenderly kissed her forehead. "I love you, too, Macy. Always and forever."

Just then, a small cry sounded in the other room.

"And that's the sound of another girl I love," Tanner said.

Macy smiled, so grateful for this second chance at love and a family.

EPILOGUE

Six months later

"I can't believe this is all coming together." Macy paused and looked around, still feeling like this day was surreal.

She stood in Tanner's grandfather's barn. It had been cleaned up. Now strings of white, twinkling lights were crisscrossed overhead. White chairs had been set up. Wildflowers decorated the edges of the rows of chairs.

In the background, a lone guitarist played a lovely melody that soothed Macy's nerves. People were starting to come in to be seated. Macy's friends from the psychotherapy center, her family. Tanner's friends from the FBI. She spotted Saul and Cara. Old friends from college had shown up even.

Macy had been able to use a portion of her savings to save Tanner's granddad's farm. Macy's sister planned on using it for wedding venues in order to keep some profit coming in to sustain the land. It was a wonderful place, full of family history. Macy couldn't think of any other place she'd rather get married.

"You ready for this?" Macy's sister, Diana, asked.

"I've been ready for this."

"Yes, you have. For a long time." Diana pushed one of Macy's curls behind her ears and smiled up at her sister. "You look beautiful."

Macy looked down at the white sundress she wore. It was simple, but she felt lovely. Tanner would appreciate the simplicity of it also. She'd never been the type to want to look fancy.

Just then, her father walked over. In his arms was Addie, who was now a year old. The girl's eyes lit when she saw Macy, and she reached for her.

"Hello, sweetheart," Macy muttered, kissing her forehead.

Addie was dressed in a matching white dress, but hers had a pink sash around the waist. A simple baby's breath headband stretched across her dark curls. She looked like a baby doll.

"You look beautiful, dear," her dad said, kissing her cheek.

"Thanks, Dad."

Someone called to him in the distance, and he excused himself for a moment.

"I'm so glad you and Dad have made up,"

Diana said, leaning close. "Maybe we can finally feel like a family. Maybe it's not too late."

"I didn't realize how resentful I was of his time with his new family," Macy admitted. "I had to reach the point of forgiveness, to realize that I was hurting myself more than I was hurting him by clinging to my bitter feelings. Besides, if Tanner could forgive me for leaving that Dear John letter, I knew I could forgive Dad."

"Well, I'm glad." Her sister gave a quick hug. "I can just feel that this is the beginning of good things for all of us."

"I hope you're right."

"I think it's time," Diana said. "The minister is motioning to us."

"Let's do this then." Macy hadn't wanted anything formal, so, against all traditions, she'd been out and about, mingling with her guests. The only person she hadn't seen was Tanner. He'd remained near the front of the barn with Devin, and Macy had stayed at the back.

As her father joined her, Macy hooked her arm through his and stepped toward the temporary staging area that had been set up toward the front. She held Addie on her hip, and Addie held her bouquet of wildflowers, pushing them up to her nose and sniffing.

As soon as Macy stepped foot into the barn, her gaze connected with Tanner's, and everything else disappeared—everything except Tanner and Addie. Tanner was dressed in his typical jeans, boots and hat. He'd never looked so handsome to her.

Her father stopped in front of the minister.

"Who gives the woman away?" Minister Harvey asked.

"I do," her father said.

Just a few months ago, those words would have caused a swell of bitterness to rise in Macy. But not anymore. Her relationship with her father wasn't perfect, by any means. But it was on the mend.

Her father kissed her cheek, and Macy met Tanner there in front of the minister.

Tanner leaned toward her. "You look beautiful," he whispered. "You both do."

Macy grinned. "Thank you. You look pretty handsome yourself."

His eyes were warm on hers, and he acted like he never wanted to look away. The realization caused warmth to spread from her gut to her heart. Today, she was marrying her dream guy. She felt like she was walking on air.

"I feel like I've been waiting a lifetime for this moment," Tanner continued.

Macy bounced Addie on her hip. "It's going to be a great day, isn't it, Addie?"

She blubbered in response and grabbed at Macy's hair.

Macy and Tanner exchanged a smile. They'd

spent every waking moment together over the past several months. Tanner was practically already a part of their family. Addie obviously thought so.

"Okay, let's do this," Tanner said. "Let's make it official. All of it."

"Tanner, Macy and Addie," Minister Harvey said. "We are here for a truly unique ceremony, but one that is filled with immense joy. It's my pleasure to bring the three of you together as a family."

"It's our pleasure to be here," Tanner said.

A chuckle swept over the audience watching them.

Minister Harvey smiled. "Tanner Wilson, do you accept both of these lovely young ladies as part of your family? Macy as your loving wife, and Addison as your daughter?"

"I do." Tanner's eyes remained latched on to hers.

"And Macy Mills, do you take this man as your lawfully wedded husband, to have and to hold from this day forward, and to be Addison's father?"

"I do." She grinned up at Tanner, her heart full of unspeakable joy.

"I understand you wrote your own vows, Tanner?"

"I did." He pulled out a piece of paper from his

back pocket and cleared his throat. "Bear with me, because I never claimed to be a wordsmith."

"Just speak from your heart, baby," Macy encouraged.

"Macy, I let you get away once, and that was the most foolish decision I've ever made. I want to spend forever with you and Addie. You both make my life better, and I wouldn't trade the two of you for anything."

Her heart warmed at the sincerity of his words. She knew beyond a doubt that he meant them. Their lives were better together. Stronger. Happier. More complete.

Addie looked over at Tanner and reached out a hand toward him. She lunged toward him, and he reached out his arms for her.

As soon as she was in Tanner's arms, Addie reached up and touched his cheek. "Da-Da," she said.

Macy sucked in a quick breath, her heart racing. "She said daddy."

It was the first word Addie had spoken. She'd had a slight speech delay, probably because of the trauma occurring in her young life.

Murmurs rushed through the audience, as well as a few cheers.

"I like the sound of that." Tanner kissed the top of Addie's head.

With her hands free, Macy grabbed her vows from the center of the bouquet where she'd stashed them, and she turned to Tanner. She didn't know why she felt so nervous. Of course, maybe it would be strange if she didn't feel a touch of nerves on her wedding day.

"Tanner Wilson," she began "I made a mistake five years ago. I'm so thankful that God has given us a second chance. I know everything happens in His timing, and despite the heartache in our past, I know that everything has worked out just as it was supposed to. You and I are meant to be joined together today…with Addie in our arms."

A huge smile spread across his face, a smile that brought such intense warmth to her heart. She wanted to make him smile like that every day for the rest of their lives. In fact, that was her goal.

"With the greatest joy, I now pronounce you husband and wife," Minister Harvey said. "I now pronounce you a family. You may kiss the bride."

Tanner stepped forward, almost as if in slow motion. His free hand went to her waist, and he tugged Macy close. Macy rested her hands on his chest, and they leaned into each other. Their lips met.

As soon as they did, Addie threw her arms around both of their necks and squealed with delight.

They pulled back and laughed, along with

their guests—their family and friends—sitting in the chairs watching.

It couldn't be a better day.

* * * * *

If you enjoyed this exciting story of suspense and romance, pick up these other stories from Christy Barritt:

*HIDDEN AGENDA
MOUNTAIN HIDEAWAY
DARK HARBOR
SHADOW OF SUSPICION*

Available now from Love Inspired Suspense!

*Find more great reads at
www.LoveInspired.com*

Dear Reader,

Thanks so much for joining me on Macy and Tanner's journey. Macy and Tanner both learn the hard truth about the pain of misunderstandings, the power of assumptions and the consequences of heartbreak. It took protecting a baby and both of their lives being endangered for their eyes to be opened to the truth.

Have you ever been in a situation you've misunderstood? Have you made decisions that you later regretted? Has God ever taken your mistakes and turned them into something beautiful and life changing?

It's funny how life can work like that sometimes. Human nature can make us prone to these mistakes. Experiences can make us view life through a lens that's not always accurate.

I'm so thankful to have a God who never misunderstands me, who knows my heart, who knows my weaknesses and who loves me anyway.

I hope you've enjoyed this story and, until next time, happy reading!

Blessings,

Get 2 Free Books,
Plus 2 Free Gifts—
just for trying the Reader Service!

YES! Please send me 2 FREE Love Inspired® Romance novels and my 2 FREE mystery gifts (gifts are worth about $10 retail). After receiving them, if I don't wish to receive any more books, I can return the shipping statement marked "cancel." If I don't cancel, I will receive 6 brand-new novels every month and be billed just $5.24 for the regular-print edition or $5.74 each for the larger-print edition in the U.S., or $5.74 each for the regular-print edition or $6.24 each for the larger-print edition in Canada. That's a saving of at least 13% off the cover price. It's quite a bargain! Shipping and handling is just 50¢ per book in the U.S. and 75¢ per book in Canada.* I understand that accepting the 2 free books and gifts places me under no obligation to buy anything. I can always return a shipment and cancel at any time. The free books and gifts are mine to keep no matter what I decide.

Please check one:
☐ Love Inspired Romance Regular-Print
(105/305 IDN GMWU)

☐ Love Inspired Romance Larger-Print
(122/322 IDN GMWU)

Name	(PLEASE PRINT)
Address	Apt. #
City	State/Province	Zip/Postal Code

Signature (if under 18, a parent or guardian must sign)

Mail to the **Reader Service:**
IN U.S.A.: P.O. Box 1341, Buffalo, NY 14240-8531
IN CANADA: P.O. Box 603, Fort Erie, Ontario L2A 5X3

Want to try two free books from another line?
Call 1-800-873-8635 today or visit www.ReaderService.com.

*Terms and prices subject to change without notice. Prices do not include applicable taxes. Sales tax applicable in N.Y. Canadian residents will be charged applicable taxes. Offer not valid in Quebec. This offer is limited to one order per household. Books received may not be as shown. Not valid for current subscribers to Love Inspired Romance books. All orders subject to approval. Credit or debit balances in a customer's account(s) may be offset by any other outstanding balance owed by or to the customer. Please allow 4 to 6 weeks for delivery. Offer available while quantities last.

Your Privacy—The Reader Service is committed to protecting your privacy. Our Privacy Policy is available online at www.ReaderService.com or upon request from the Reader Service.

We make a portion of our mailing list available to reputable third parties that offer products we believe may interest you. If you prefer that we not exchange your name with third parties, or if you wish to clarify or modify your communication preferences, please visit us at www.ReaderService.com/consumerschoice or write to us at Reader Service Preference Service, P.O. Box 9062, Buffalo, NY 14240-9062. Include your complete name and address.

LI17R3